1

The Rule of Proposals

As the wind was blowing, I placed my hand on the collar of my coat.

Dropping my gaze from the sky, I noticed a young girl standing beside me on the empty tree-lined street.

'Yuzuru Kamiya-san?'

Shocked to hear my own name, I croaked, 'Huh?' and took a good look at the girl standing before me.

This wasn't the first time I'd been stopped on the street. I was an actor, and despite my lack of experience, I had been signed with a management agency and was already starting to book steady work. If my face was recognizable at all, I'd say it was to kids in her age group, as I was starring as one of the live-action superheroes on Sunday morning television.

The problem for me was *how* the girl addressed me.

My name was Yuzuru Kamiya, yes, but kids usually

referred to me by my superhero colour, Blue, or my character name, Kanata. So I wasn't used to being called my full name, and with the honorific *-san*, no less.

'. . . Yes?' I said to the girl.

Was she in first or second grade? She had refined features and a confident look in her big, brown eyes. Her face was tiny, her jawline sharp. Light eyebrows. Her chestnut-tinged hair was pulled into two curly pigtails and tied with ribbon, and her bangs were parted in the middle to reveal a smooth, shapely forehead.

When I think of children, my mind goes straight to the professional child actors I work with on the show. And like those I meet on set, this girl seemed mature for her age.

We were in a park encircled by high-rise office buildings in the Hibiya business district, situated across the street from a bar-lined neighbourhood. Until today, I had no idea this park even existed. I'd never been in the area on a weekday while the sun was still up, and the daytime energy took me by surprise. The park brimmed with mothers pushing strollers and office workers who were apparently taking extra-long breaks.

'Um . . . and you are?'

I knew I had the right place and time, and I'd been waiting for a while. But the person I'd been on the lookout for, the person I imagined I'd be meeting today, was much

How to Hold Someone in Your Heart

www.penguin.co.uk

Also by Mizuki Tsujimura

Lonely Castle in the Mirror
Lost Souls Meet Under a Full Moon

How to Hold Someone in Your Heart

MIZUKI TSUJIMURA

Translated from the Japanese by
YUKI TEJIMA

doubleday

TRANSWORLD PUBLISHERS

UK | USA | Canada | Ireland | Australia
India | New Zealand | South Africa

Transworld is part of the Penguin Random House group of companies
whose addresses can be found at global.penguinrandomhouse.com.

Penguin Random House UK, One Embassy Gardens,
8 Viaduct Gardens, London SW11 7BW

penguin.co.uk

Penguin
Random House
UK

First published in Great Britain in 2025 by Doubleday
an imprint of Transworld Publishers

Originally published in Japanese as *Tsunagu Omoibito no kokoroe*. All rights reserved.
Publication rights for this English edition arranged through Kodansha Ltd, Tokyo

002

Copyright © Mizuki Tsujimura 2019
English translation copyright © Yuki Tejima 2025

The moral right of the author has been asserted

Typeset in 12.35/16.5 pt Adobe Jenson Pro by Falcon Oast Graphic Art Ltd.
Printed and bound in Great Britain by Clays Ltd, Elcograf S.p.A.

The authorized representative in the EEA is Penguin Random House
Ireland, Morrison Chambers, 32 Nassau Street, Dublin D02 YH68

A CIP catalogue record for this book is available from the British Library

ISBN 9780857529664

older – definitely not a girl carrying a pink frilly purse. She seemed to have come alone. *She had to be one of my fans. Right?*

I was about to flash her my brightest actor smile when she said, 'Shall we go?' She turned and started to walk away.

'Um . . . sorry. I'm meeting someone here.'

'I know. I'm the person you've been waiting for.'

I blinked.

'I'm the go-between.'

She began to walk away, and I followed. 'I – I heard that you could arrange meetings?'

She turned around, trained her wise-looking eyes on me. 'I bring together the living and the departed. That's what a go-between does.'

I imagined for a second that I was watching a child actor perform. She spoke in a voice as clear as day, and in a daze, I listened.

SHE LED ME to a cafe in the basement of a shopping plaza just a short walk from the park. It was one of those old-fashioned coffeehouses with a glass display by the entrance lined with plastic replicas of coffee, cream soda and other menu items.

In an area that seemed to be unveiling one new sparkling shopping centre after another, I wondered why I was being led – by a child – to an old coffeehouse in an old-fashioned building, but I kept my mouth shut. The coffeehouse was mostly empty but for a few customers – long-time regulars, no doubt. We were easily the youngest there. The newspapers and literary journals stacked in the magazine rack by the door did not cater to a young clientele.

The girl chose the seat farthest from the entrance – normally reserved for the guest of the party – and regarded me with a smug stare. I got the message and took the chair opposite.

'So . . .' I said, cowering ever so slightly under her glare. 'Are you really the go-between? I had heard that it was someone older. I'm pretty sure the person who picked up my call was an adult.'

I only half-believed the rumour about the 'go-between'. Supposedly, these were people who could help reunite you with a loved one who had died. But you only had one chance. The first time I heard the story was at a cast party for a play that had just ended its run.

'Hey, has anyone close to you died?' a cast-mate had asked me after a few too many drinks, not expecting a serious response. 'If you were given a chance to see that person again . . . would you want to?'

Assuming his go-between story was nothing more than an urban myth, I started bringing it up casually with people. *Have you heard of the go-between?* Most reacted with amusement, as I had, but there were some who didn't seem to find it funny.

One cast-mate I knew only vaguely came up to me at a different party. 'I don't know if you should joke about it. Some people might not be into that kind of thing, but more than that, I wonder if you want people thinking *you* are.'

Her tone wasn't rude or forceful, which is why I actually considered what she'd said. In this industry, it was true that being viewed as super religious or dependent on 'unseen powers' could raise some eyebrows. I stopped bringing up the go-between.

Who knew that a few years later, I'd be running around trying to track down the go-between myself?

The young girl scowled at my question. 'If you're not going to believe me, I can just leave now.' She regarded me suspiciously. 'How did you find out about the go-between anyway?'

'Uh, I'm an actor, and uh, an actor friend told me about it.' I waited for her reaction, but the word 'actor' didn't seem to stir up any emotion. Part of me scoffed, *Don't you know who I am?* while another part of me laughed at my easily bruised ego. 'At first I thought it was an urban myth, but then I started to look into it . . . and well . . . I finally decided to call.'

When I dialled the number, a guy who sounded about my age picked up, or so I'd thought. And the posts and comments I came across online had said the go-between was an elderly person, all of which made me wonder if the go-between was really a large-scale organization that ran psychic scams. Perhaps the phone number I'd found was some kind of trap. I came to today's meeting vowing to leave as soon as I sensed something even slightly fishy. But now that I was sitting face-to-face with a small girl, I had no idea what to think.

'Hmm,' she murmured, looking as though she wasn't listening, or couldn't care less even if she was. She pointed at the laminated menu. 'I'll have a cream soda. You?'

'Uh, sure, I'll take one too.'

At that moment, a man who appeared to be the owner set two glasses of water in front of us. We ordered two cream sodas. 'Sure thing,' he said with an unhurried languor that made me think, now *this* is more like the go-between I was imagining.

'What do you know about the rules?' the girl asked once the owner was out of earshot.

'I have a general idea. But it'd be great if you could give me a rundown. Is it true that you can, uh, talk to dead people?'

'I don't *talk* to dead people. I set up meetings,' she stated. 'If you're thinking of channelling, like the mediums on Mount Osore do, you're wrong.'

'Channelling?'

'I don't let dead spirits possess my body and I don't pass messages on to the living. I set up a meeting between you and the deceased person you wish to see. I'm strictly the go-between.'

She sounded as though she were reciting from a script again. I had to focus all my energy just to keep up with her.

'Um, OK. So you people put us in touch with whoever we want.'

'You people?' She cocked her head.

'Uh, I figured there were a few of you. Aren't you an organization?'

'No. There aren't a few of us. I told you, I'm the go-between,' she grimaced. 'Let me finish explaining. The go-between receives a request from a living person, someone like you. You tell me about the person in your life who has passed away. I take your request back with me and present it to the departed. I confirm whether they would like to see you too. If they say yes, I set up the meeting.'

'OK.'

The go-between. When I first heard about them, I

remember thinking that they sounded a lot like the Mount Osore mediums the girl mentioned.

I'd heard rumours about big-name politicians getting advice from notable historical figures, and celebrities having teary encounters with friends who'd died too young. They were basically fairy tales for adults. But in some circles, the go-between was a known and regular presence, as common a rumour as business moguls and stars paying large sums for a psychic or an astrologer. Whether someone can find their way to a go-between depended on three factors. One, that you know they exist, two, that you believe they exist, and three, luck.

'When you say you arrange for us to meet, do you mean . . . um, what *do* you mean?'

The girl eyed me as though I were a mystical creature. *You came here without knowing that?*

'I mean, what about their bodies? Dead people are cremated and don't have bodies. Right?'

'They will appear looking just as they did in life.'

The cream sodas appeared before us. 'Here you go,' the owner said. The girl stopped talking long enough for him to set a coaster and drink in front of her, along with a long spoon. She unwrapped the spoon curled in a thin paper napkin and made a prayer gesture before starting in on her soda. I joined her, and the two of us sipped wordlessly from our artificially coloured lime-green drinks.

The girl turned her eyes up at me and continued, her mouth still on the straw. 'The spirit of the deceased is permitted to take on a physical form when at the location designated by the go-between. The living person can see them, of course, and also reach out to touch them.'

'I don't believe it,' I heard myself say. The girl ignored me and poked at the vanilla ice cream floating in her drink. 'How is that even possible?'

She let out a long sigh. 'Isn't that why you came to see me? If you don't like it, you can always go somewhere else. Yes, you get to see the person, actually talk to them. What more do you want?'

'I don't know, it's just so unreal. Our world connecting with . . . the other one.'

'You make your request, and I relay it. Whether the deceased accepts or not isn't up to me, but I will negotiate to the best of my ability,' she continued in her clerical tone. The gap between her crisp, articulated sentences and the knitted ribbon dress and fluffy mouton boots was widening every second.

'First, I need to know their name and the date they passed away.'

'Oh, I'm not the one who needs a meeting,' I said as her eyes bore into mine. 'I came today because, well, I have this friend. I was hoping you could help reunite her with someone she really needs to see.'

Hadn't I already explained this in my phone call?

Ever since I first heard about the go-between, I'd been thinking . . . This didn't apply to me, of course, but maybe some people in the world *did* need for them to exist. That was why they'd continued for so long, wasn't it?

And I had someone like that in my life. Somebody for whom time seemed to have stopped because of some incident in the past.

'I'm here to ask for a meeting on her behalf,' I said, hoping to sound serious. 'Can you set up a meeting between my friend and her best friend who died?'

MISA AND I met two years ago when we were cast in the same play.

We were both just starting out, and although we weren't the leads, we'd played a couple, which meant we spent a lot of time together rehearsing. We kept in touch after the show closed.

My start in show business was nothing remarkable. Ever since I was a kid, I'd always loved being the centre of attention, and after being told I had the looks and the magnetism, I got it into my head that I was born to be a star. I auditioned for all the top entertainment agencies and got rejected from every single one, until I somehow made it to the final round with my now-agency. The guy who'd actually been selected had to drop out at the last minute, which was how I was chosen.

Even though it wasn't the sensational star-making debut I'd dreamed of, I started to play tiny parts and found the acting work to be more invigorating and fulfilling than anything I could learn at school. I'd always been a terrible student, but as I threw myself into the craft, people started to see me as dedicated and hard-working. I felt I'd finally found something that might give my life meaning.

I said yes to every job offer that came my way, mainly in theatre, and if I heard there was a new movie or play with a character that resembled a role I was playing, I was first in line to see it. I usually walked out of the theatre feeling humbled and overwhelmed, but knowing I wasn't half as good as the actors I'd just seen, I felt I had nothing to lose. Let the other actors run circles around me. My ambition was insatiable, and I wanted to learn from the best.

Gradually, I started landing TV roles that were more than walk-on parts, and when I was offered the role of a superhero in a TV show for kids this past spring, I was so overjoyed I called my mother in tears.

I'd flung myself into the industry without much thought or research, and I knew I was fortunate to have made it this far at all. In fact, people often commented on my 'incredible luck', both as a compliment and not.

Misa was my opposite. She was the type of actor people might call 'serious'. She had enrolled in acting school as a teenager and studied the craft for years, then gained theatre experience working backstage for a famous theatre group before signing with her current agency. When we first met, she wasn't widely known, and even today, her occasional appearances were for small, unmemorable roles. She had complete command of her facial expressions and body – I didn't even come close – and yet she was offered so few onscreen roles. I wasn't sure if it was something about her acting style as a trained theatre actor, but it was a shame, nevertheless.

Misa and I could talk all night. Time flew by when I was with her. I'd never been much of a book reader, aside from manga, but she shared a few titles that I actually found engaging. The first time I read a novel from cover to cover, I was so proud of myself that I called her in the middle of the night. I couldn't help it.

'This is huge! You don't understand, I always thought I was an idiot. But I did it, I read a book!'

'You called to tell me that?' Misa sounded exasperated, but I thought I detected a bounce in her voice. 'OK, let me try to think of some other books you might like,' she said, and in that moment I knew I was into this girl.

The next time we hung out, I told her how I felt and asked if she would go out with me. I knew what people thought of me – shallow, dumb, a player, whatever – but I was serious about Misa and had genuinely worked up my courage to ask. But she laughed me off and said, 'You're kidding, right?'

It was around the time I'd got the superhero role on TV.

'This is an important time for you, and there's still so much *I* need to learn about acting. Now's not a good time for either of us, don't you think?'

She was right, of course. But I thought she enjoyed being with me as much as I did her. The possibility of her turning me down had never crossed my mind.

'Is there someone else?'

I pictured Misa with some other guy and felt myself grow hot with jealousy.

'It's nothing like that.'

Then what? My chest filled with anxiety. I'd never been flat-out turned down by a girl before.

'Do you want me to wait? Until we're older, my career's on track, and you're happy with the work you're doing. You're not going to date until then, is that what you're saying?'

She looked surprised that I hadn't simply replied 'OK' and walked away. I realized how shallow I must have appeared in her eyes and felt deflated.

'The answer will probably always be no, no matter how long you wait. I'm not allowed to be happy.'

It sounded as though she'd let that slip.

'Huh?'

'What I mean is, I have to be grateful to be doing what I'm doing. I can't expect to have an amazing personal life too. Can't have everything, right?' She turned her mouth up into a vague smile. 'You're a good person, Yuzuru, and you can do better.'

If she'd told me she just wasn't interested, that she couldn't see us as more than friends, I might have had an easier time accepting it.

And then one day—

I went to see Misa in a play, and when I visited her green room after the performance, I ran into some of her classmates from high school. 'Oh my god, is that Yuzuru Kamiya?' one of them whispered when she saw me.

While Misa caught up with other guests, I introduced myself and started talking to her friends, searching for the opportunity to casually ask, 'Did Misa go out with anyone back in school?' Maybe she was reluctant to date because of something that had happened in a past relationship.

'Hm, I don't know,' one of her friends said. 'She was always so focused on acting.'

'There was a time, a long time ago, when she was more

easygoing and boy-crazy, but all of that changed,' another friend said. 'Now she's like, obsessively driven.'

Misa didn't seem to hear us. Her friends then lowered their voices to tell me about Misa's best friend, who had died during high school. And how, since the accident, Misa had stopped smiling and laughing, squealing over boys.

'They were inseparable. Practically twins. When I look at her now . . . she looks like she lost her other half.'

If only there was a way for them to see each other again.

'THE BEST FRIEND died on the scene, apparently. There was no time to say goodbye. I found the newspaper article. Would you like to see it?'

As I was explaining, I noticed the girl hadn't said a word. She blinked her large, round eyes and slowly exhaled.

'I hate to have to stop you,' she said. 'But the go-between can only take requests from the person who wants the meeting. You are not permitted to make requests on their behalf.'

'Huh?'

'Can you tell your friend to contact me directly?'

'No, you don't get it.'

Sensing that the girl was about to get up and leave, I

half-rose from my seat. 'She's not the type to believe in stuff like this. She's super realistic, and like, rational and smart.'

'Sounds like you're saying people who come to the go-between are irrational and dumb.' The girl narrowed her eyes.

'But . . .' I rasped, needing to keep the conversation going. 'I tried to bring it up with her once, and she didn't look at all interested. I mean, I don't blame her. That's why *I'm* here. I figured the best I could do was to bring her friend back and sit them down together.'

'Even so, if your friend has no desire to meet, then I can't negotiate with the deceased. That's just how it is.'

'But they do have a chance to meet, right?' I didn't mean to yell. The girl flinched, and I felt the stares of the other customers, but I didn't care. 'If there's even the smallest chance she might reunite with this person, I want to help. Please. Can't you do something?'

'OK, calm down.' The girl furrowed her brows, looking all grown-up again. I wondered what kind of household she was raised in. 'So let me get this straight,' she said, leaning forward and looking me in the eyes. 'You want to help her.'

'Yes.'

'So she'll be grateful, and she'll owe you, and hopefully, she'll go out with you. Is that right?'

'Uh—'

'Right?'

'Wrong!'

That was my best comeback. As I sat there stupidly, the girl took out a notepad with a cartoon bear on the cover.

'I just want to help her work out her regrets.'

'There's no guarantee that a meeting with the deceased will help someone work out their regrets. Anyway, rules are rules. If your friend wants a meeting, she needs to meet me herself. Unfortunately, even if you pass her my details, I can't promise we'll be able to connect. Some people call countless times and can't get through, while others who were meant to connect often do so without trying. Whether or not a meeting is in the cards for your friend has nothing to do with you.'

'I don't get it.' I didn't mean to sound bitter, but none of this made sense. 'Then how come I got through so easily? Especially if you're just going to turn me down.'

'That's the weird thing,' she said, tilting her head quizzically. 'Requests like yours generally don't get through. It's a mystery to me too, which is why I came to see you.'

'Aw man, I wish you could have just told me all this over the phone. I'm busy too, you know.'

This is my first afternoon off in forever, I thought, covering my face with my hands. The girl slurped her cream soda wordlessly. My own glass was now a sloppy blend of soda and melted ice cream, but she'd been expertly making her way through and was about to polish off her drink.

'Talk to your friend again. She can then decide what she wants to do. Remember, this is about her, not you. Why don't you stop thinking about how you're going to get her to go out with you?'

'I *told* her about the go-between!' I retorted. 'But not only did she not believe me, she started to look at me like I couldn't be trusted. Fine. What if *I* met up with the best friend?'

The idea had just come to me, but it wasn't half-bad. I'll meet with the friend, in Misa's place. She would probably know why Misa had become such a different person after the accident.

'You can if you want,' the girl said with a sigh and put her chin in her hands. 'But what makes you think she'll want to see you too?'

'What?'

'Let me finish explaining the rules.'

She flipped a page in her notepad and scanned it.

'You can request a meeting, but the deceased has the right to decline. I will take your request and pass it on to the deceased, after which they will decide yes or no. If they say no, that's the end, unfortunately.'

'But the girls were best friends. If I say I'm a close friend of Misa's, I might have a chance.'

'Both the living and the dead have one opportunity for a meeting. The departed can meet with one living person only.'

'What? So if they've already met with a family member or something . . .'

'They can't take any more requests.'

'Oh . . .' I felt as though the rug had been pulled out from under me. 'So, say I do meet with this person . . .'

'Then she won't be able to see anyone else. If your crush decides somewhere down the line that she wants to make a request, you'll have used up the opportunity.' The girl didn't mince words. 'The deceased must be careful about who they say yes to, because it's their only chance too.' She lifted her gaze. 'Also, we . . . the go-between is not able to take requests from the dead. Which means the deceased can only wait, hoping the living person they want to see will request them.'

'OK.'

'So, if the deceased is hoping to be summoned by someone specific . . . are you ready to barge in and take that chance away?'

'. . . No.'

'Same goes for you.'

'Me?'

'If you meet with the best friend now, you won't be able to make another request.'

'We have one chance here, and one chance there.'

'Correct. If your request is denied, however, it won't be counted against you. The rule applies only when both sides agree, and a meeting transpires. Otherwise you're free to request someone again.'

'So you're saying it's not easy.'

'Just remember that there's no guarantee you'll connect with the go-between later. Like I said, it's preordained.'

'Even just sitting here with you now is starting to feel like a miracle.'

The conditions were uncompromising, but maybe there was a reason for it. If people were allowed easy access to both worlds, they would flock to see their loved ones, and if that happened, death would cease to have meaning.

'I wonder if she's already seen someone. She died so young. Maybe her parents.'

'I'm not at liberty to give out information about other requests.'

This entire consultation seemed like a wasted effort, so I said irritably, '*Of course* you're not.'

'What would you like to do? Do you wish to continue?'

'No, that's OK. I can't take the opportunity away from someone who might actually need it.'

The little girl didn't seem bothered about my disappointment.

'OK,' she said. With nothing left to say, we stared at our

drinks in silence. My ice cream had completely melted into my soda now. I mixed it and sipped through my straw.

I watched as the girl closed her notepad and put it neatly away. Then she asked, 'It's a little weird for you to be drinking that, don't you think? I thought adults drank coffee.'

'Some do. But I like my drinks with ice cream.'

'Oh.'

Her usual clients probably didn't order cream sodas. I slurped down the rest of my drink and felt the sugar rush through my tired brain. I had a shoot scheduled later in the day.

I offered to pay for the sodas, but the girl declined. She whipped out a cutesy wallet from her purse and started to pay. Since all I could do was watch, I decided to step out of the cafe and wait.

The girl walked out of the cafe and gave a curt 'Bye'. As she was about to walk away, I blurted out, 'Uh, since you're here . . . and all . . . can I make a request?'

The girl looked at me in disbelief. But I was aware I might never see her again. *Might as well use this opportunity.*

'My dad's dead . . . I mean, my parents got divorced a long time ago, so I didn't know him or anything but . . . do you think you can set up a meeting? If possible.'

The girl let out a loud sigh.

'Why are you bringing this up *now*?'

'Sorry,' I said. She glared at me and dug in her purse for the notepad. Opening up a new page, she thrust it at me along with a pen.

'His name and date of death?'

'Ichiro Kumada. I think he died . . .' I searched my memory and scribbled the date in my chicken-scratch handwriting. The girl watched me curiously.

'What?' I asked.

'You have a dead father, but all you could think about was making a request on behalf of the girl you like? Seeing your dad never occurred to you?'

She didn't sound exasperated, just genuinely curious. 'Yeah,' I laughed sheepishly. It was true. When my cast-mate asked if anyone close to me had died, I'd answered, 'Nope,' without thinking twice. My dad never crossed my mind.

There are people in the world who need the go-between. I just wasn't one of them.

'And why would you like to see him?' the girl asked. 'Now that you've brought him up, I will do my job. So?'

'Uh—' I hadn't thought about it. 'I guess . . . well, I've never met him, so I want to see what he looks like. And he treated my mother like dirt. I want to give him hell for that.'

I never expected to see him while he was alive, and I don't know why I wanted to see him at all now. But when I realized I had just one opportunity, I suddenly didn't want it to go to waste. And for some reason, he had popped into my head.

'OK,' the girl nodded as though she didn't care one way or the other, then closed the notepad.

'Oh, the money.' I almost forgot. 'How much do I owe you? If the meeting happens, but also in the event that it doesn't.'

I thought briefly of cancelling my request if it cost too much. I'd heard rumours about it being a few million yen, tens of millions in some cases.

'Oh,' the girl nodded. 'We don't take money.'

'Huh?'

'It's free,' she said. 'This is like volunteer work.'

'Seriously? I heard it would cost several million. Can you just tell me up front? I don't want to get a huge invoice later.'

'I told you, it's not necessary.'

'But—'

'Do you want to pay? Free isn't good enough?' She put her notepad away irritably. 'I'll get back to you after I hear your father's answer.'

'OK.'

'Bye,' she said, turning her back for good this time.

In a flash, she was gone.

*

THE NEXT MORNING started early.

'And *cuuut*! OK, let's break.' The director's voice echoed throughout the studio.

The child actor shooting with me was having a rough day. Normally a breeze to work with, today he was flubbing his lines and missing his mark in action scenes.

Hayata was only seven, and nearly in tears, which didn't happen often. His mother came over to him. Watching them out of the corner of my eye, I put on my bench coat and took a sip of coffee. We all forgot our lines at one point or another, and the mood on set wasn't particularly tense. 'How about taking an early lunch today?' someone suggested. Hayata's mother bowed apologetically to the cast and crew.

Sana Mishiro, otherwise known as Pink Ranger, grabbed a baked *taiyaki* cake from the catering table. 'Hayata, want one?' she said. The boy's eyes lit up. 'Thank you. I would like one,' he enunciated clearly, which impressed me and made my heart twinge a little.

Hayata was a better-known actor than me, having recently risen to popularity in a hit prime-time TV drama series. 'I really liked your show,' I told him the first time we met, to which he'd replied without missing a beat, 'Thank you. I couldn't have done it without the support of people around me.' And he'd bowed. The words flowed out of him like lines he'd perfected, and I'd felt shut down. He approached everybody on set in the same polite manner.

'I'm sorry, Kamiya-san,' he said, apologizing for flubbing his lines.

'Don't worry 'bout it,' I smiled and threw him a peace sign. He only bowed again, his expression serious. I thought he interacted more naturally when the cameras were rolling.

The girl I'd met yesterday was also smart and articulate, but there was something different about her. No one seemed to have taught her to be that way.

I watched Sana nibbling on her *taiyaki* next to Hayata, her tanned legs stretched out under her miniskirt, and thought about how cute she was. It was only after I'd been cast in the series that I learned Misa had auditioned for the part of Pink. That had been her last shot, as the age limit for television roles was often lower for female actors.

'Wanna get lunch?' someone said.

It was Takasugi, also known as Black.

'Let's do it.'

The studio where we were shooting was famous for its cherry blossoms, though the trees were completely bare now. The tree-lined path and small stream next to it was open to the public, which meant there was often a crowd hoping to catch a glimpse of filming.

As we walked out of the studio, we heard, 'Hey, Kanata!'

and 'Hey, Black!' and turned to see two preschool-age boys making our trademark poses, their expressions fierce. 'Hey there!' Takasugi waved, and it wasn't the boys, nor their mothers, but the teenage girls next to them that squealed. 'Thanks for coming!' I waved both arms.

We walked into the cafeteria, bought meal tickets for the daily special and found a table. I was finally growing accustomed to seeing famous people I'd only seen on TV before, eating lunch here like regular folks. I'd learned to feign nonchalance, though inside I still hollered, *Oh man, that's so-and-so!*

The cafeteria was emptier than usual, and we found a table by the window. As we sat down with our trays, my phone vibrated. I saw *Go-Between* on the screen and said to Takasugi, 'Sorry, gotta take this.'

'Hello?' I said, hurrying to a corner of the cafeteria.

'Hello, this is the go-between.' The girl. 'I'm calling about yesterday's request. Your father says he will see you.'

I swallowed what felt like a block of air. My immediate reaction was, *Of course he will. Who else is gonna request him?* He was a drunk and a cheater. There was no chance of anyone else wanting to see him, now or in the future.

'*Huh.* Wonder if he knows I want to punch him in the face,' I spat out.

'You can ask him that when you see him.' She continued

in a clerical tone, 'You will be able to meet through the night, for one night only. Normally from around seven in the evening until dawn, which is around six o'clock this time of year. The meeting will take place at a hotel in Shinagawa.'

She named the date and time. Two weeks from now. My schedule was in my phone, which I couldn't check now. 'If that day doesn't work, I'll call back with a different date. In that case, it will be about a month later.'

'I'll check my schedule and get back to you. Is there something special about that day?'

'It's the full moon.'

'Oh.' I guess it made sense. The moon and the go-between seemed to go hand-in-hand.

'You can meet the longest during a full moon. OK then, please get back to me once you've checked your schedule.'

She hung up.

I looked up and saw Hayata standing at the entrance with his parents. His tears had dried, and he was holding his father's hand. His dad scanned the room and commented with a smile, 'Big cafeteria.' The family was holding bento boxes and found an empty table without buying meal tickets.

I returned to our table where Takasugi was halfway through his daily special.

'Look,' he grinned, pointing at Hayata's table. 'He laughs like a kid when he's with his dad.'

'Yeah, even though he's way more mature than us,' I too laughed. It was a relief.

MY DAD WAS gone before I understood what that meant.

When I was in elementary school, I pestered my mother with questions. *Why don't I have a dad? Why is our family just you and me? What kind of guy was he?* She didn't seem to want to share much, but I did know that he was alive, somewhere in the world.

Kids can be cruel. If he was going to be gone either way, I thought he might as well be dead. In TV dramas, being separated by death made a touching story, but there was no good emotional hook about a dad who was alive but just didn't want to be with his family.

My mother might not have talked about it, but the people around us sure did. He was a gambler. Deep in debt. Deadbeat. Alcoholic. Womanizer. Who knew why women found him attractive? I once heard, 'A woman came charging into their house with a knife!' I'd shuddered at the thought.

When my parents were first married, my father worked as a 'real estate broker', whatever that meant, and for a time, he was rolling in money. But he got caught up in a questionable land development project that bankrupted his small company and landed him in debt. In the months and years that followed, he spiralled out of control, making no attempt to find new work. When he became physically violent towards my mother, she was left with no choice but to leave him, taking me with her.

'There was a time when Mah-chan believed that having a baby might change him, but that didn't happen,' a relative once said. Mah-chan is my mother's nickname; her given name is Mahko.

The relative had meant no harm by the comment, but I was a teenager then, and what she said tormented me for years.

My mother worked from early morning to late at night at a bento shop owned by someone she knew. Her hands were chapped and cracked all year long, and she wore no makeup. Still, she was beautiful. The prettiest by far of all the parents who visited our school on class observation day.

My cheating, no-good father had dumped the burden of raising a child on my mother. And that's exactly how I saw myself. As a burden. Baggage. It was because of me that she couldn't remarry and start her life over. I spent much of my adolescence brooding, and my mother picked up on it. She would say to me, 'I'm so glad you're here with me, Yuzuru. When your father and I divorced and I was suddenly on my own, you are the reason I was able to get through it. I have you, and that's all I need.'

When I mentioned baggage, she cried, '*Baggage?* Are you kidding me? You're my hope. Whatever happened between me and your father has nothing to do with you. I may not love him any more, but I love you. So much.'

As a teenager, I was horrified by phrases like 'I love you' and 'You're everything to me'.

Now, my mother's words mean the world. They had illuminated my path.

My mother and I had no interest in where Dad was or how he was doing, until she received a phone call three years ago in winter.

'Yuzuru, it's your father,' his mother said when she called me to relay the news. 'He's dead.' She didn't sound sad, at least not that I could tell.

He had died at home, alone, from a heart attack. His landlord found him almost one month after his heart stopped. A dismal ending to a sad life.

My mother was notified by my father's relatives – just in case, they said – and she informed them that she would attend his memorial services. 'I know you're busy,' she said to me. 'And your father was from Hokkaido, which is where the service will be held.' She seemed to be telling me in a roundabout way not to join her.

When she returned to Tokyo after the funeral, she

excitedly laid out the souvenirs of Hokkaido ramen, crab and other local delicacies. 'I did so many touristy things!'

I hadn't asked about Dad since I was a child. He was someone she'd had to flee, after all. But I asked if it had been painful to attend his funeral.

She laughed and said, 'He's dead. I have nothing to be afraid of any more, so no, it wasn't painful. His family gave me this when they went through his things. Take it if you want.' She handed me a brown vinyl figurine shaped like a fish. I didn't have the faintest idea what it was, but she said it was a fishing lure. 'He really loved to fish,' she murmured. That was the first time I'd heard anything about him aside from his being an incompetent loser.

'Nah, that's OK.' I set the lure on the desk.

My mother now lived alone in the house where I grew up, and I could smell incense in the air. As she turned to hang her funeral dress by the window to air it out, I noticed she was no longer smiling. Though she insisted that she was just tired from the flight, her eyes were sunken in like she'd been crying.

I'd never even seen a photo of my father. Never felt the need. If he ever asked to see me, the answer would have been no. But he never did, and now he was dead. I had no desire for a face-to-face, but the idea that he'd not wanted to see *me* infuriated me.

I made a fist and bit down hard. *The selfish jerk. Up and dying without thinking about anyone else.*

For the first time in my life, I wanted to see him.

I wanted to see him and punch him in the face.

I HAD ONCE been for a photoshoot to the five-star hotel in Shinagawa, where the meeting would be held. I was new to show business then and even less known than I am now, but the hotel employees had treated me like royalty, and I remember shrinking in their presence.

Tonight was a full moon, like the girl said, and the winter air was crisp and clear. I stepped into the hotel with the moonlight on my back.

The soaring ceiling and winding staircase of the entrance hall were no less intimidating on this night. With its polished deep green marble floors, impressive pillars, and a vase of flowers that would take several people to carry, the place was made to be photographed.

The girl was already here. She saw me and stood up from her chair, then headed my way. 'Shall we go?'

'This hotel is insane,' I said, slightly nervous. I couldn't imagine how much a night's stay cost. Being here made me feel the way I did when I was taken to an expensive restaurant where the food was served in courses. Guilty that Mom couldn't be here to enjoy it.

'Are you sure I don't have to pay?' I asked as we walked towards the elevator. The girl ignored me. I was about to repeat my question when she said, 'Your father's already here.' I shut up. 'Room 1207 on the twelfth floor. I'll go up, but I won't be joining you. Take all the time you need.'

'. . . OK.'

'Please come find me in the lobby when you're done. I'll be there waiting.'

'You're going to wait up all night?' My eyes widened. Was a child allowed to sit alone in a hotel lobby throughout an entire night?

'It's my job,' she said.

Was the go-between a career? I felt uncomfortable hearing a kid her age call something a job.

'No need to worry. I can take care of myself.'

'OK. Um . . .'

'Yes?'

An empty elevator arrived, and we stepped in. Leaning on the wall, which was actually a window with a full view of the lobby, I suggested, 'You know, if you want, I can get you an autograph.'

'Huh?'

'No, uh, not just mine. If there's an autograph you want,

I can get it for you. I'm on a superhero series right now. You might not care, but is there anyone at your school that might? I feel bad about not paying for this meeting. If there's anything I can do, you know . . . I work with Hayata too, if you want me to get his autograph.'

'No, thank you,' she said icily.

The elevator reached the twelfth floor, and I felt a drop in the pit of my stomach. *I'm here.* My pulse started to race.

'Here's the key.' She dropped a small paper envelope into my palm. 'Good luck.'

The elevator doors closed. As I stepped on to the plush carpet, I wondered if I was crazy for doing what I was about to do. I swallowed, then started towards the room. I turned a corner and arrived in front of a room at the eastern end of the hotel. I took a deep breath.

It occurred to me then that I'd never seen my father before, and I wouldn't be able to tell if someone was impersonating him. For reasons I can't explain, knowing that soothed me a little. Maybe the girl had found an actor to play my dad. I probably wouldn't be able to tell one way or the other, but the idea that he might be a fake lightened the load a little.

I knocked twice. 'Yes,' said a voice from inside, clearer than expected. I took a breath and turned the knob.

*

THE ROOM SMELLED like alcohol. I hesitated before taking a small step forward.

You're drinking, man? I felt wild disappointment. I hadn't come with high expectations, but wow, he was just like everyone said. This was no impersonator. This loser needed to drink to get through the night. This loser was my dad.

That girl's for real, I thought. She had really brought my father over from the other world.

He was in front of the desk. Not sitting in a chair, not even perched on the bed. He was kneeling on the carpet with his knees together, looking right at me as I walked farther in. His eyes bulging, his face frozen in fear. When he saw me, he opened his mouth.

'Are you . . . Yuzuru-san?'

San?

He wore a pair of old white slacks and a tattered button-down shirt that looked like it hadn't been washed in days. He had the appearance of a man who couldn't hold down a job. Suddenly, he leaned his upper body forward and lowered his greying, close-cropped head to the carpet.

'Thank you for making time to see me. I am . . .' He swallowed before croaking, 'Ichiro, your father.'

I was caught off-guard. I'd come prepared to punch the guy in the face, and the last thing I expected was for him to bow at my feet. 'Uh yeah,' I stammered. The man, whose

body was folded like a grasshopper, kept his head lowered.
I wondered if he was going to stay that way until I said
something.

'I'm . . . Yuzuru Kamiya.'

The man still didn't lift his head.

'Uh . . .' I wondered if he was messing with me. I raised
my voice irritably, 'Um, hey.' But then I saw his hands, which
were clutching the carpet. They were trembling. His nearly
bald head was shaking, and something was dripping on to
his hands – tears, saliva, snot, a mix of all three – as he tried
to contain his sobs.

The old man was crying.

'I'm sorry. I'm sorry,' he whispered.

I was about to reach for him but stopped and took a deep
breath instead. On the side table sat two empty, crushed
beer cans.

Had no idea dead people drank. I was strangely impressed.
'Dad,' I said aloud for the first time. The word just slipped
out.

When he heard it, he let out a long wail as though he
could no longer keep it in. 'I'm sorry. Please forgive me. I'm
so sorry,' he cried.

I grabbed his shoulders and forced him to lift his face. I
was physically stronger than him now. He turned his cloudy
eyes towards me, and when our eyes met, he started to cry

again. 'Yuzuru,' he repeated my name, without the honorific this time. The shape of his eyes looked a lot like mine,
drooping at the corners. This was him. The coward who
couldn't face his son without the help of a few drinks. True
to form.

HE CONTINUED TO sob, and I made him get up off the
floor and into a chair at least. I waited until his breathing
calmed. After a while, he peered at me gingerly and asked,
'OK if I get a look at you?'

'Yeah.'

I took a seat in a chair across from him. I didn't need for
this guy to grovel and wished he would get it together. My
chest tightened momentarily, and I found it hard to breathe,
though I couldn't explain why.

'You look just like . . . Mah-chan. How is she?' he asked.
I learned for the first time what he had called my mother.
I thought about the smell of incense in the house, her back
as she hung up her dress.

'She's fine.'

'. . . Good.'

We were out of things to say.

The moon shone outside the window. I gazed at the man

sitting before me, his shoulders hunched. He didn't strike me as a violent-looking person, though he *was* undoubtedly the washout everybody said he was. How could this guy be a womanizer? If he had some kind of irresistible charm, I didn't see it.

His twig-like fingers squeezed the fabric of his trouser pockets, and he finally broke the silence. 'How old are you?'

'Twenty-three.'

'I see. You're not ... married yet, are you? Or what, do I have grandkids already? What about work?'

'I'm not married. And yes, I work.'

Unlike you, I wanted to say. *And even if I did have kids, you have no business calling them grandkids.* I knew the old man was dead and I was being petty, but I couldn't help how I felt.

He looked at the floor. Still, he tried to keep the conversation going. 'What made you want to see me?'

'It wasn't you I wanted to see originally. Things just kind of turned out this way. What I *wanted* to do was reunite my girlfriend with someone she knew. But then the go-between girl said she couldn't take my request ...'

'What, you have a girlfriend?!' I hoped he'd be hurt that he wasn't my first choice, but he didn't seem to have noticed. 'What's she like? Is she pretty? Is she like your mother at all?'

I'd called Misa my girlfriend, which was of course untrue.

'Yeah, she's beautiful. She's an actress.'

'An actress? You're kidding me.'

'No. I'm an actor too.'

My father's eyes widened. 'You're kidding.'

'Not kidding. I'm in a TV series.'

'No! You have anything you can show me? Anything. A magazine cutout, a movie poster?'

'I have some photos . . .'

I took out my phone and pulled up some images. As I started to turn them towards him, he grabbed my phone and said, 'Look at that!' and wrapped both hands around the device as though it were a treasured possession. 'It's you. Yuzuru . . . what do you know. I'm impressed.'

'I was going to become so huge one day that you would regret ever leaving us.'

My father turned his sunken eyes towards me. His face was gaunt, like a skeleton, and devoid of colour. Is this how he looked when he died?

'Mom had such a hard time raising me alone. If I ever saw you, there was one thing I wanted to ask you. I get why you'd think you could never show your face again, but still, didn't you want to see us? Even once in your life?'

'Of course I did.'

'Why'd you die without coming to see us?'

'. . . I was scared.' He pursed his lips, which made him look like a child. 'When we split up, Mah-chan told me never to come near you two again. I put her through so much, I didn't think she'd ever let me see you and apologize.'

His eyes wavered.

'Huh. You wanted to apologize. Didn't think you had it in you.'

I couldn't seem to get a sentence out without it sounding accusatory. Tonight was all I had with the guy. I knew I'd regret it if I continued on like this, but I couldn't help it. 'I heard you were a drunk and a cheater. And you were up to your eyeballs in debt.'

My father stared at the floor. 'That's what I've been told since I was a kid, which is why I can't enjoy a drink, or even place a dumb bet on something. I'm scared that I take after you.'

It was true that I was cautious about drinking and gambling. But what I was most concerned about was the relationships.

'You don't know this, but I've always been popular with girls. Since I was a kid.'

'I'm sure that's true. You're a good-looking boy.'

'It scared me to realize that if I wanted to, I could prob-ably go out with a lot of different girls at the same time and be fine with it. Knowing that about myself disgusts me. It makes me think of you. I don't want to be anything like you. You're like a damn curse.'

The first time I realized my fear was when Misa turned me down. I'd never asked a girl out and been shot down before, but I felt as though she saw right through me.

'I'm a curse, huh?'

'Yeah, you are. Do you know how hard you've made Mom's life?'

After he'd separated with my mother, I heard the old man never remarried, going from gig to gig doing manual work, and spending his daily earnings on alcohol.

'Why'd you marry Mom if you knew you were going to make her miserable?'

'Well, that's easy. Mah-chan's not like other women.'

He looked down helplessly, but when he saw that I wasn't going to offer any help, he started to explain.

'. . . I wanted to raise a family with her,' he said, then looked away again as though he was embarrassed by what he had to say. 'I wanted to see how she would care for our kids, what kind of mother she would be. I was in love with your mother.'

'But you weren't around to see any of it. Because you couldn't hold it together.'

'Yeah,' he nodded, but he didn't shrink this time. To my astonishment, he smiled. 'But you know what? It worked out. Looking at you now, I can tell your mother did an incredible job. It's like a slap in the face. Thanks, Yuzuru. For being by her side all these years. Now that I've met you, I can tell she's doing well.'

What right do you have, I wanted to yell, *to even think those things after you walked out on us?* But then I remembered my mother's words.

I'm so glad I have you, Yuzuru.

She was the reason my chest felt constricted. My eyes welled with tears, but I tried to brush them away before the old man could notice. 'Whatever,' I said.

'But seriously, wow . . . you're an actor. And you're on TV? Who'd have guessed it.'

He fiddled clumsily with the smartphone, flicking back and forth between the photos of magazine articles and play-bills with my name and headshot on them.

He held the phone with both hands as though he were praying. 'Look at you . . . Yuzuru . . . an actor.' I noticed he was crying again. 'I wish I could have raised you with her. I wish we could have been a family.'

'And why couldn't we? Whose damn fault is that?'

I bit my lip and jabbed his side as he sat curled like a piece of shrimp. I'd come ready to slug him, but my fist only made soft contact with his skinny ribs.

'Thanks . . .' he said through sobs. 'Thanks for coming to see me. I didn't expect to ever see you again.'

'It's too late for that, man. You're dead.' I gave him another sock in the side.

He lifted his tear-stained face and laughed. 'I forgot about that.'

He gave a goofy grin. It showed no despair.

'She's not really my girlfriend,' I confessed with the help of a beer.

It was after midnight, and my father was still clutching my phone, now sticky from his fingerprints. I pointed at the photo of Misa and said, 'She turned me down.'

'What? That's pathetic!' My father slapped me on the back. Harder than I expected, with that skinny arm. 'So she rejected you once. So what? If you like her, you keep trying. Keep trying and keep trying, to the point where she takes pity on you. That's how I was with your mother.'

'And then you made her miserable, so what was the point of that?'

'That's true. I made her life hell. But I was so happy to be with her.'

I couldn't believe this guy. How self-centred could he be? He even sounded *proud*.

'I am genuinely sorry for the way I treated your mother. But marrying her was the best thing that happened to me, and if she hadn't married me, you wouldn't be here. Am I right? Listen. If you want to propose, this is how you do it. You offer everything you've got, I mean, you go all out. If you believe you can make her happy, you don't hold back. Don't worry. You're a good man. Good-looking too.'

'Yeah, whatever.'

This guy couldn't lift his face off the ground earlier. He'd been trembling, calling me *Yuzuru-san*. I wanted to run and tell my mother that.

The eastern sky was gradually growing lighter. I was surprised to have spent an entire night with my father, whom I couldn't have picked out of a crowd before tonight.

'I'll tell Mom about this someday,' I said. 'She'll never believe me about the go-between, but when her time comes and she joins you up there, you better go to her and beg, I'm talking *grovel* for her forgiveness. And who knows, someday I might come join you guys too, maybe with my own family.'

I still wasn't entirely sure whether the 'other world' existed, but I felt I'd gained a better understanding of why people believed in heaven. Knowing there was a chance for a reunion in the future provided people with something to hold on to. My mother and I would find each other again, might one day catch up with this old man too.

It wouldn't kill us to have a little hope.

My father looked as though he were choking up again.

'We never lived as a family here, but if we run into each

44

other over there, let's surprise Mom. Show her we know each other.'

'What are you talking about? We lived together as a family. I took you fishing!' Tears formed a layer inside his pale eyes.

'Huh?' I replied. 'Oh yeah.'

We'd lived with this man until I was about two. Though I never knew he took me fishing. I'd been captivated by the fish-shaped lure, he told me, swinging it around and hiding it in my boots.

'You were a cute kid.'

'I know I was.'

He recalled a time when I nearly fell into the ocean. And the time I *did* fall into a fishing pond. I'd started splashing around, he said, screaming with laughter. 'You had no fear,' he remarked.

The stories continued for the rest of the night, and the mood never turned dark again. When the sun came up, the chair he had sat in all night went cold. He was gone. The only thing left behind was my phone, which was still open to the poster of a play Misa and I acted in together. The morning light lit up our faces.

*

I RODE THE elevator down to the lobby and found the girl waiting on the sofa. She saw me and stood, looking the same as yesterday with her purse hanging off her shoulder.

'Finished?' she asked, looking neither sleepy nor tired. The antique grandfather clock near the entrance pointed to six-thirty. Early departers in suits rolled their suitcases past us.

'Yeah.'

The go-between still felt surreal, though much more real after my meeting.

'Thanks,' I said, returning the room key. She took it without a word. 'I'm glad I made the request. We drank the beer in the fridge. You're sure it's OK?'

'Yes. Goodbye,' she replied, then started to turn and walk off.

'Hey,' I called behind her. 'Are you sure I can't sign an autograph or something? Do you want to come watch us shoot an episode? Is there any way I can pay you back?'

She was probably too old for superhero shows and obviously not interested in an autograph, but I was desperate to give her something.

'No. You really don't have to.'

'OK then,' I said, trying to hide my disappointment. 'I'll get really famous. I have a good movie lined up. I'm gonna work hard and become so mega famous that you'll definitely want my autograph.'

I didn't expect the girl to take me seriously, but her expression wavered a bit. 'OK.' Our eyes locked for a moment, before she looked away. 'I'll look forward to it.'

'Thank you.'

I bowed my head deeply.

I was about to leave the hotel when somebody slipped through the door, nearly running me over.

'Oh, excuse me.'

'No worries,' I said, raising my gaze. I thought I saw the person catch his breath.

'Oh, uh, sorry, are you Yuzuru Kamiya?'

The guy looked to be about my age, maybe a little older. He was wearing a pretty cool coat, its leather and fabric design reminding me of a coat I'd worn in a fashion shoot this past winter.

'I am.'

He didn't look like someone in the industry, but he was tall with sharp, good-looking features.

'Oh wow, I'm a big fan. I can't believe my luck, running into you like this. I hate to bother you, but would it be all right to ask for an autograph?'

'Um . . . really?'

After being treated like a nobody by the little girl, I had to admit his request made me smile.

As I signed a page in his notebook, I wondered if he had a child who watched my show. That would make him a very young father, but it wasn't impossible.

Taking my autograph, he bowed his head and thanked me.

'See you,' I waved.

'Thank you, really. Have a safe trip home.'

Have a safe trip home? When leaving a hotel, didn't people usually say, *Have a nice day?* It wasn't until much later that I realized it was strange for the guy, who wasn't even a hotel employee, to be sending me off at all.

I CALLED MISA on my way home from the hotel and asked her to meet me later at a park near her house. When she said she was busy, I promised it would only take a minute.

I then called my mom and swung by her house. 'I'll take the thing,' I said, retrieving the ratty old fishing lure.

I asked if she remembered me playing with the lure as a kid. 'Not really,' she shrugged. Still, she had selected this item from all of my father's belongings. And he hadn't thrown it out in the first place. The tiny item was proof that they had once shared a life together.

'Did I ever fall into a pond?'

To that she shook her head firmly. 'No. But your father did. You were pointing at him and howling with laughter.'

'What's up? Why the sudden call? Aren't you busy?'

'Not today.'

Misa scanned the surroundings, making sure nobody was around. She always worried about walking too close or being seen alone with me, though no paparazzi was interested in my personal life.

'Um . . .'

'Yeah?'

Misa looked at me with those striking eyes.

Though I wasn't sure she would believe me, I decided to tell her all the things that had led up to my meeting with my father. I didn't care if she felt sorry for me. And then, I would ask her what had happened in her life. What had happened that still haunted her today? Whatever it was, I was confident that we could overcome it together.

'I saw the go-between.'

Misa stopped, her large eyes widening. She'd once told me, 'I don't know if you should joke about things like that,' and I expected her to brush it away again. But this time, she nodded. 'OK. How was it?'

'Uh, fine, I guess.' I remembered the little girl's smug

expression. Misa murmured something. I thought I heard her say, 'Was he still wearing the coat?'

'Huh?'

Misa took a deep breath, then lifted her gaze.

'Who was your meeting with?'

'. . . My dad.'

She didn't rush me. She simply looked at the ground and said, 'Want to come over?'

It was my turn to open my eyes wide.

'I want to hear your story. But I'm telling you now, my place is tiny.'

'Are you sure?'

'Be warned. It's a mess.'

'Hey, Misa,' I said, touching her arm as she started to stand. If I missed this chance, I thought I would never say it. She turned and saw my face, which was frozen in fear, and burst out laughing. 'Yuzuru, you're such an open book. I was always envious of you for that.'

'Huh?'

'Do you remember the first time we were alone together?'

'Uh . . .' I tried to remember but couldn't.

She laughed. 'Bunka Theatre in Shinjuku. We were meeting up to see a play, but I got lost and was wandering around the lobby when you yelled my name and waved from the second floor balcony. *Misa, up here!*

Now that she mentioned it, I did remember. Misa's face relaxed into a smile.

'Here you are, this popular actor, screaming my name across the lobby. Not even trying to hide your face. You didn't care what people thought. I was horrified, but also a little touched.'

I didn't know where she was going with this, so I stayed quiet. 'Let's go.' She reached out her hand. 'I want to hear about the go-between and about your father. Tell me everything. I want to talk to you about something too.' Then, 'It might make you hate me,' she murmured. She said it casually, but I heard. I bit my lip and took her hand. It was soft, cold and small. I squeezed it.

'Tell me.'

'WAKE UP.'

The car approached the Akiyama house and made a right turn at the corner. Anna, who had been asleep in the passenger seat, woke with a start, her notebook slipping out of her arms. Ayumi replaced it. 'Wake up, we're almost home.'

'I'm so sleepy,' Anna grumbled. She pried her eyes open. 'Isn't it against the law to make a child work through the night? I'm going to remember this, Ayumi. You owe me big time.'

'Aw, come on, it was just this once.'

'Well, since you *did* get me his autograph, I'll forgive you. A little.'

She happily patted the notebook with Yuzuru's autograph inside.

Ayumi sighed. 'If you like him so much, you should have just asked him yourself. Got him to shake your hand.'

'No. The go-between can't do that.'

Anna was eight this year. She was too old to be into superhero TV shows, but this season was different because a child her age was in the main cast. The kids at school all watched the show every week.

'This was a special case. I stepped in to help because you said the client was Yuzuru Kamiya, but I can't do this every time, you know. Please do your own job. The go-between is your responsibility.'

'Yes, ma'am.'

After the death of Ayumi's great-uncle Sadayuki, this little girl, Anna Akiyama, was named the new head of the family. Sadayuki had specified as such in his will. Anna was his great-granddaughter and still a small child when he appointed her.

A few years after that, Ayumi's grandmother passed away,

but the Akiyamas continued to treat Ayumi as one of their own. They supported him, both professionally and privately, as had been his grandmother's wish. And Anna had led the way.

'But why couldn't *you* take this case on?'

'It just . . . seemed complicated.'

He'd been shocked to hear the request on the phone.

Hi, my name is Yuzuru Kamiya, and I have a request, but it's not really for me. It's for a colleague, no, a friend. Her name is Misa Arashi, and she's an actor. Have you heard of her? She lost her best friend back in high school . . .

He hadn't heard the name in years. But not a day passed as the go-between when Ayumi didn't think about Misa Arashi and her friend. The memory of them throbbed like a splinter that had never been removed.

Ayumi hadn't seen Arashi since high school. They now lived in different towns, and he'd assumed their paths would never cross again. Misa Arashi had already used up her one meeting to see her best friend. It was one of Ayumi's very first cases as the go-between.

He could still remember her screaming.

Let me go! Back to Misono, one more time. I just need a second!

Yuzuru Kamiya had called to say he wanted to make a request on her behalf, but Ayumi knew that Misa was out of chances. Though of course he couldn't tell Yuzuru that.

'I'm glad though,' Ayumi said. 'It sounds like she's doing well.'

He had seen some of Arashi's work in years past, and he kept an eye out for any TV appearances.

'Hm,' Anna nodded. 'I hope things work out for them.'

'Yeah.'

'Hey, vapour trail!'

Anna pointed to the brisk winter morning sky, where a white cloud stretched in a thin straight line. Ayumi cracked his window open to let some air into the heated car. A sharp chill pricked his skin.

He was about to begin his seventh spring as the go-between. Seven years had passed since he'd taken over from his grandmother.

2

The Rule of Historical Research

'No one but me is silly enough to make a request like this. Am I right?'

The man leaned in, the bootlace tie around his neck swinging forward and back. He wore thick glasses and a linen shirt, and he was busily wiping the beads of sweat from his forehead with a handkerchief.

Ayumi sat across from him in the museum cafe. 'Uh, sure,' he said, taken aback by the man's gusto. As he scanned the room to see if people around them had heard, the man continued, not wanting to lose him.

'Anyone who thinks about requesting a historical figure has either not thought it through, or they think it's all fun and games. Nobody in their right mind actually wishes for something like this. I, however, am different.'

*

AYUMI'S MORNING STARTED most days by going into the office of Tsumiki no Mori, the company where he worked, based in the stylish Daikanyama area.

'Good morning.'

The office was small, holding just seven desks, and every time he opened the door, he was welcomed by the soft scent of hinoki cypress.

He'd joined the wooden toy manufacturer after college and was now in his second year as a product planner of handcrafted toys. The company rarely hired new employees, and Ayumi expected to be the youngest staff member for at least a few more years. Though junior staff members were often expected to arrive before their bosses, at this company, the president, Imura, was usually in before him.

'Morning, Ayumi.'

As usual, Imura was reading the newspaper with a cup of tea he had poured himself.

Their company distributed wooden toys to a handful of speciality toy stores in Tokyo. They were selective about how their products were made and distributed, and they were known and respected in the industry for their attention to detail.

Ayumi first came across the company when Anna was a newborn and he was looking to buy her a gift. He'd walked into a toy store and found himself drawn to the warm colours and touch of a wooden puzzle. When he took the puzzle home, his grandmother picked up the box and said, 'Oh, I know the studio that made this. Your father once designed furniture with them.' She squinted at the name on the label. 'My goodness, it's been a long time.'

Ayumi's father had died young, and it was rare for his grandmother to talk about his professional work as an interior designer.

He took note of the company that distributed the toy: Tsumiki no Mori. The Forest of Wooden Blocks. A few years later, when he started looking for a job out of college, he noticed that the company was hiring. Ayumi had studied art and design in college – a path he believed was unrelated to his father – and was interested in the product design for a wide range of items including toys.

Only after he joined the company did he bring his father up in a conversation with the president. He was quickly put in touch with Torino Workshop, the family-run woodworking studio that had made the wooden puzzle. The husband-and-wife team greeted him warmly the first time he visited their studio in the woods.

'We're so happy for the chance to work with both father and son,' they said, which meant more to Ayumi than they knew.

The wooden puzzle he had given to Anna was solved

long before she reached the recommended age. Ayumi next gave her a disentanglement puzzle, also made from wood, which even he found challenging. But she solved it again in no time and said, 'Buy me the next one as soon as it comes out, OK?'

Ayumi's company had only a handful of staff members and was swamped during certain times of the year. As a second-year employee, he was constantly learning and apologizing – hardly what one might call an asset to the company. But this year, he had come up with a product idea that had got the go-ahead from his boss.

'Ayumi, are you going to Torino Workshop today?' Imura asked.

'Yes, they called and said the samples are ready.'

His boss smiled. 'There's nothing like that moment you see your first product on store shelves. I still remember it. And when you see someone buying it? No words.'

'I'll probably cry when it happens,' Ayumi laughed. He checked his email one last time and stood up from his chair. Grabbing his coat, he said goodbye and was on his way.

He got off the train at Karuizawa Station, about a seventy-minute ride from Tokyo, then transferred to a bus that drove through groves of paper birch trees. When he stepped off the bus at a stop near the studio, he closed his eyes and inhaled deeply, imagining the fresh clean air entering his lungs.

Ayumi savoured his walk from the bus stop to Torino Workshop. Strolling along the narrow path, he noticed the forest trees were richer in colour and fuller in their scent compared to just a month ago. It was still cold enough in Karuizawa in May to require a coat, but even under chilly skies, he could feel from the lightness in the air that winter had passed.

As he walked, his phone rang. He stopped and reached into his bag to pull out a flip phone that he carried separate from his smartphone. It had belonged to his grandmother, and he had it set up so calls to his house would automatically transfer over. It hadn't rung in a while. Someone was calling from a landline with an area code he didn't recognize.

'Hello?'

'Hello,' said an older man. 'Is this the phone number of the go-between? I heard that, er, you can set up meetings.'

'Yes, that's correct.'

Ayumi wondered if he sounded any more mature than when he had first started as the go-between while in high school. Clients were often surprised when he used to show up to a meeting. 'But you're a *kid*,' many said in disbelief.

Sunbeams shone through the openings of the trees. He raised his eyes and squinted, checking to see that nobody was around before continuing, 'You've reached the go-between. We set up meetings between the living and the dead.'

Not everybody knew that the go-between existed, and whether someone found their way to him was a matter of fate. That was what his grandmother always said. Those who did find their way reached the cell phone in Ayumi's hand.

In the years since he'd taken over the role, Ayumi had learned how rare it was for a request to actually come to fruition. He'd assumed people would flock to the go-between, but his phone seldom rang. Few found his phone number, and even if they did, there was no guarantee that Ayumi would be able to pick up. When he called back, he often found the caller couldn't be reached. And they almost never called again.

But a small percentage rang when he could take the call. Of those calls, he went on to set up three meetings at most each month. Because the meetings were said to be best during the full moon, Ayumi often scheduled one or two meetings on the same night. Some months passed without a single request. This had been the case when he was in high school, college, and now, as a working adult. Which was why the job wasn't ever a burden on him or on his elderly grandmother, when she had once been in the role.

Once he took over, the Akiyamas had said that he could make the go-between his full-time job if he so wished. They were a family of fortune-tellers with a long, prominent history and could support him. But Ayumi couldn't imagine asking them to support him for work that only transpired once or twice a month, and he had politely declined. He needed a regular job. Needed to stand on his own two feet.

The caller introduced himself as a former educator from Niigata Prefecture.

He had been the principal of a local high school, a post from which Ayumi guessed he had retired years ago. He seemed to have difficulty enunciating at times, but he spoke very politely, for the most part.

When asked if he could meet in person to discuss the request, the man replied, 'I assume the meeting will take place in Tokyo. Are you familiar with the library inside of the Sengoku Museum in Ueno?'

'No, I'm sorry, I'm not. But I'm sure I can find it. Would you like to meet there?'

'Across from the library is a cafe that serves delicious *anmitsu* desserts. The coffee's quite good as well. Let's meet there. It will be my treat.' The man wasted no time.

Ayumi gave a small laugh. 'Thank you.'

He hung up and noticed that in a matter of ten minutes,

the sun had moved higher and now shone more brightly. Such a nice day, he thought, stretching his arms towards the sky.

As Ayumi approached the studio, he smelled fresh wood that was distinct from the trees in the forest. He heard the low roar of a power scroll saw and the pounding of a wooden mallet. As he poked his head into the log cabin-turned-studio, the owner appeared from the garage. 'Hey, you're here.'

Torino Workshop was a small family-run business. Ayumi referred to the husband-and-wife team in their late fifties as *Taisho*, an affectionate and respectful term for Boss, and *Okusan*, a friendly term for Mrs Boss. Their daughter Nao, who handled administrative duties, was their only employee.

'Shibuya-kun? Are you here already?' Okusan said as she rushed out of the studio, wiping her hands on her work apron. She wore a bandana around her head. 'My goodness, you must have left Tokyo early this morning. I apologize for the mess. We don't even have tea ready. Nao! Nao!' she called out.

'Oh please, don't worry about me,' Ayumi insisted.

The owners had been long-time acquaintances of Ayumi's father, and they treated him as though he were part of the family.

'You didn't drive today?' Taisho asked, peering behind

Ayumi. 'We have a few samples for you to take home. They might be heavy to take back on the train.'

'My boss took the car today, but I'm sure it won't be a problem. I can handle it. Thank you so much. You made different versions of the sample? I can't wait to see them.'

'Let him in, Dad,' a voice said from behind Taisho. A slender hand appeared in the doorway and their daughter Nao appeared wearing a red check apron. 'Welcome, Shibuya-san,' she smiled.

When they first met, she'd struck Ayumi as a poised, beautiful woman with bright eyes. She worked just as hard as her parents, treating their clients with great care, and many considered her to be the face of the business. Though she was three years older than Ayumi, she always addressed him politely by his last name.

'Hello.'

'I apologize for my family. They're always so loud when you visit.'

'What's wrong with that?' Taisho pursed his lips in what looked like a pout, making Ayumi laugh. He and his daughter seemed close. 'But Ayumi, you really should have brought the car today. We were going to have you take back some fresh vegetables too.'

'Thank you! And I will get everything home, whatever it takes.'

They stepped inside the studio, where Ayumi spotted a chair that his father had made.

'We use it so much. I'm sorry for how beaten up it looks,' Okusan apologized, showing him the chair with the gentle curves, the small scratches on the back, the sunburn marks.

'It's great as a chair, but also makes the perfect impromptu table,' Nao added.

Gazing at the chair illuminated by sunbeams from the window, Ayumi felt in a way as though he were reconnecting with his father. He loved being here.

NOT ONLY HAD Ayumi not known about the library and cafe inside the Sengoku Museum, he was not aware that the museum existed until today.

He arrived late Sunday afternoon and was surprised to find children and families milling about the museum and library. The cafe, on the other hand, was occupied by elderly folks poring over thick reference books. For them this wasn't a lazy Sunday visit with friends and family; they appeared absorbed in heavy-duty research.

The man sat in a high-ceilinged space of the cafe with his eyes glued to the entrance, which was how Ayumi knew it was him.

'Excuse me, are you Samekawa-san—'

'Oh, are you here on behalf of the go-between?' the man cut him off.

'Uh, I am the go-between, actually. I'll be the one taking your request.'

'Oh, is that so? All right then. Thank you.'

The elderly man wore thick glasses and a bootlace tie from which hung a marble-like ornament, and his shirt, though slightly worn, was buttoned to the top and tucked neatly into his trousers. He looked how Ayumi imagined a former school principal would.

'May I hear your story? After which I have a few rules I need to go over with you.'

'Fine. But first things first. I promised you.'

'Excuse me?'

'My promise. That I would treat you to *anmitsu* and coffee.'

'Oh.'

Ayumi wasn't hungry, and he was hesitant about being treated by someone he was meeting for the first time, but Samekawa had already gone up to the counter and was placing his order.

He appeared to be around seventy. His trousers hung loose on his thin frame, but he stood on sturdy legs. He returned to the table holding the receipt. 'Sorry to keep you waiting,' he said, taking a seat. 'I couldn't help ordering one for myself. Anyway, thank you for meeting me. The name of the person I wish to meet is—'

'Um, just a moment, please.'

Ayumi had to stop the man before he took control of the entire meeting. The old man paused, looking surprised.

'May I first explain the rules of the go-between? I'm obligated to explain them to you.'

'Oh, is that so?' Samekawa sat up straight. 'Of course. Go right ahead.'

Why did this client feel different from the others? Ayumi wondered, then immediately knew. Most of the people who came to him had a bewildered air about them, as though they couldn't decide if he was actually real, whether they were being conned. Ayumi's first task was often to explain patiently what the go-between was.

He clarified that he didn't call up dead spirits like the mediums of Mount Osore, that the deceased appeared looking as they did in life, and that both the living and the dead had only one chance for a meeting. Ayumi tried to be as empathetic as possible when sharing the information, trying not to overwhelm anyone.

But aside from the occasional 'Mm-hmm' or 'I see', Samekawa seemed to have no reaction. Ayumi's explanation went so smoothly that he started to worry if he was getting through to the man.

'The dead will appear as they did in life, and you will be able to reach out and touch them. The meeting will take place over a single night. Any day of the month is fine, but we recommend the night of the full moon. That is when you are able to meet for the longest.'

'Fine,' Samekawa nodded. 'The date you decide on is fine. Now, may I tell you my story?'

'Uh, yes ... sure.'

Samekawa didn't seem to have any doubts about whether the go-between was real.

'You're very young,' he said, looking at Ayumi. 'Have you ever heard the name Uekawa Gakuman?'

'No ... I'm sorry. I haven't.'

'I see. Well, I don't blame you. Were you born in Tokyo?'

'Yes.'

'I see, I see.'

Ayumi braced himself for a lecture about not recognizing an important historical figure, but Samekawa only nodded proudly. 'He's a legend in my hometown. When people think of Niigata Prefecture, they think immediately of the all-too-famous samurai lord, I'm sure you know the one, who overshadows everyone else. You see, Gakuman was just a low-ranking official, the head of a farming village.'

'Um, do you mean like *shoya* in old legends?'

'Shoya!'

Ayumi thought he'd come up with a pretty good example, but Samekawa raised his voice as though he couldn't believe what he was hearing.

'*Shoya*, or village headmen, were born much later, during the Edo Period. They were the highest-ranking of the three types of village officials ... and yes, Uekawa Gakuman's lineage does later become *shoya* in the Edo Period, so you're not wrong. But Gakuman was from a different time. I don't think they were called *shoya* back in his day.'

'Right.'

Ayumi decided that he would keep his mouth shut while the man told his story. Samekawa cleared his throat and readjusted his seat, as though he'd been interrupted.

'Gakuman lived during the Feudal Era, or Sengoku Era, before the Edo Period. His region was ruled by the famous samurai lord. They were constantly at war with neighbouring regions.'

Ayumi wondered who the 'famous samurai lord' was that Samekawa kept alluding to, but he was afraid to interrupt again. He tried to picture the map of Japan and recall what he'd learned in history class. 'Can I safely assume that you know who the famous samurai lord is?' Samekawa asked, as if he'd read Ayumi's mind.

'Uh, actually, um . . .'

Samekawa looked up at the sky and took a deep breath. 'Heavens! The Feudal Era? Niigata Prefecture? It can only be Uesugi Kenshin, right?'

'Uh, right.'

Samekawa gave an exaggerated sigh. 'When you don't know the answer, it's fine to say that you don't know. It's better to ask questions than to say nothing at all.'

'I heard you were a schoolteacher,' Ayumi said. 'Did you teach history?'

'No, I taught Japanese. Classics were my speciality. But this is common knowledge for anyone from the region.'

'Oh, I see,' Ayumi said, though he didn't know what he was agreeing to.

Their coffees and desserts arrived. Ayumi was shocked by the size of the cream-topped *anmitsu* dessert and suddenly became worried about finishing it.

'Let's eat,' Samekawa said, picking up his spoon. While Ayumi hesitated, the old man plunged in. The man, it appeared, had a sweet tooth. 'During the Feudal Era, many villages were ruled by the farmers themselves, or else low-ranking lords such as Gakuman. This was during a time when the warlord Uesugi Kenshin was launching into battle with neighbouring lands, and soldiers were needed. More and more, everyday farmers were going to war and often coming back war heroes. They achieved a higher status, and the longstanding line separating the elite samurais from lowly farmers was starting to waver.'

'Right.'

'The reason I hold Gakuman in such high regard is ...'

Samekawa carried a spoonful of sweet *kanten* gelatin to his mouth and swallowed. 'He didn't send anyone from his village to war. Not a single one. As the war escalated between Uesugi Kenshin and Takeda Shingen in the Battles of Kawanakajima, nearby villages sent countless men to combat, but Gakuman refused. He ignored orders to deploy his men, saying, "I will not send anybody from my town."'

'Wow,' Ayumi said.

Samekawa didn't seem satisfied with his response. 'Do you know what that means? What a tremendous thing that was to accomplish? We're talking about a time in history when people born into the lower ranks of society were finally given the chance to overthrow their superiors. Until this era, people who were born farmers lived and died as farmers, but those who became heroes in battle were given medals and higher positions. Going to war was an *opportunity*. For young men, especially second and third-born sons who were of less value to the family than the eldest sons, to resist the temptation to go to battle took enormous strength and courage. I imagine that many in his village must have protested his decision, yet Gakuman didn't waver. He protected the lives of his townspeople.'

'I see ...'

'And that is quite a feat.'

The old man poured milk and sugar into his coffee and drank it loudly. 'He must have been viewed by many as a traitor. It wasn't until much later that he was recognized for his achievement. I might say it was a recent development, from a historical standpoint.' He set down his spoon and looked at Ayumi. 'This Uekawa Gakuman is of great interest to me.'

'I see ...'

'I grew up hearing heroic stories about Gakuman from my parents and grandparents, and I continued my research of his life and career in my years as a teacher, visiting historic sites, delving into the region's history.'

Ayumi finally understood what the man was saying.

'You would like to meet with this Uekawa Gakuman ... san.'

'That's right.'

Samekawa bowed his head deeper than he had all day. 'I will owe you a tremendous debt.'

*

MEETING WITH THE deceased usually meant reuniting with a person with whom one had a deep connection in life. Family members, best friends, respected teachers, beloved partners . . .

The only case Ayumi could recall of a client requesting someone they'd never met before was his first as the go-between, when a woman had asked to meet a celebrity she admired deeply.

He didn't know what to say. After a long pause, he asked, 'I understand your request. Though I cannot promise that Uekawa Gakuman will agree to meet with you. Um, he died in . . .'

'The fifteenth year of the Tensho Era. The same year Toyotomi Hideyoshi completed the construction of the Jurakudai palace in Kyoto. Gakuman was the head of his village until shortly before he died. He had no children, and he left what little he had to his younger brothers. His final years were spent in quite humble surroundings, I hear.'

Ayumi could not begin to fathom when the 'fifteenth year of the Tensho Era' was. Seeing his bewilderment, Samekawa said, 'It's 1587. Record shows that he passed away on September the seventh.'

'So . . . over four hundred years ago . . .'

'Yes,' the old man nodded. 'Is this your first time getting a request of this kind?'

Ayumi thought at first that Samekawa was asking about the difficulty of his request. But then he noticed that the man looked thrilled. 'No one but me is silly enough to make a request like this. Am I right?' The man leaned in, the bootlace tie around his neck swinging forward and back.

'Uh, sure,' Ayumi replied, taken aback by the man's gusto. As he scanned the room to see if people around them had heard, the man continued, not wanting to lose him. 'I'd say anyone who thinks of requesting a historical figure is doing it for laughs, or else it's a fleeting thought. Nobody in their right mind would actually wish for this. I, however, am different.'

He felt overwhelmed by the request, but Ayumi also understood the man's excitement. He'd thought about it before too. A chance to meet with the dead opened up the possibility of seeing someone from another era. He could think of a few legends he would love to connect with in person. But whether he would use his one opportunity was a different story. People didn't search desperately for the go-between for a one-on-one with a stranger.

Which was exactly what this elderly man had done. Eyes sparkling, he asked, 'You're very young, but has there been anyone like me in the past? Someone whose wish was to meet a historical figure?'

'Not that I know of. I think many have the idea, but few actually go through with it.'

Ayumi wondered why this man's request had made its way to him at all.

'Oh,' nodded Samekawa, appearing slightly let down. 'So nobody's quite dumb enough to request it. What a shame. I was going to ask you how things turned out.'

'I'm not sure about "dumb". You yourself are requesting a historical figure.'

'Oh no, it's different with me. I've come fully prepared. The people I call dumb are those who think they can just meet up with someone from hundreds of years ago without any preparation. People wishing to meet Murasaki Shikibu, who wrote *The Tale of Genji,* or the powerful samurai Oda Nobunaga, simply because they feel some kind of affinity.'

Ayumi doubted that Murasaki Shikibu or Oda Nobunaga would accept the requests, but he kept his thoughts to himself.

Did the go-between exist during their time? He didn't have a clue. Even if they had, Murasaki Shikibu and Oda Nobunaga were actual legends; certainly they had used their one meeting already. Not to mention that even historical figures, when given the chance, would probably prefer to see a family member, partner, or somebody close to them in life.

Ayumi couldn't imagine that they would travel through time to say hello to a fan.

'Say they do meet with a historical figure,' Samekawa continued. 'Chances are, they'll end up regretting it. First of all, these historical figures communicate in a different language from what we now use. It will be like speaking to someone from another country.'

Huh, Ayumi thought. He'd never considered that before. He remembered that Samekawa's expertise was in classic Japanese literature. And yes, the Japanese of classic texts from centuries ago was unrecognizable from the modern language spoken today.

'Even in the same country, languages evolve over the course of several hundred years. People nowadays watch TV dramas and manga and see historical figures speaking contemporary Japanese, and they mistakenly assume that they will be able to communicate. So silly. And quite arrogant.'

'. . . Right.'

Ayumi felt as though he were being lectured. Samekawa looked pleased to see Ayumi nodding.

'For example, *Hyakunin Isshu* is a famous poetry collection that has been around for centuries, and though we are familiar and often read aloud from it, our cadence and pronunciation are said to differ greatly from when it was first written. There is a recording of the collection in its original pronunciation, compiled by researchers and academics. You should give it a listen. It's quite fascinating.'

'What does it sound like?'

'How do I explain it . . . it's unrecognizable. It almost sounds as though they are joking around.'

'Wow. But how did people figure out how the words were pronounced back then? If no one has ever heard it.'

'Listen . . . the thing you're asking me to explain is the very research that academics have devoted years of their lives to,' he said, sounding peeved.

Ayumi was only curious about the preservation of sounds at a time when no recording devices were available, but Samekawa must have taken his curiosity for nitpicking.

'Anyway, the person I wish to meet is Uekawa Gakuman, the man who once headed the region where I still live today. I come from a line of farmers who were able to live out their lives because of the decision that he made. If he had allowed his villagers to go to war, I might never have been born.'

'And you would like to express your gratitude?'

'Of course. But more than anything, I am a life-long researcher of Gakuman,' Samekawa said proudly. 'I grew up hearing stories of his heroic actions, and have been reading about him and studying his life since I was a young man. Over the years, I've given talks about Gakuman alongside university professors, and I also work as a guide at the local museum.'

'Right.'

'I have made a commitment to learning about him. And yet, there remain two mysteries that I have been unable to solve.'

'Mysteries?'

'Yes,' he said, his eyes twinkling. 'The first has to do with his decision to keep his villagers at home. Forbidding his men to go to war, going directly against the orders of the feudal lord Uesugi, seems to be a reasonable choice from a modern pacifist perspective, but it could only have been seen as foolish back then. I imagine he was called a coward and a traitor.'

'Right.'

'What made him think that was the right choice? His thinking was too modern for his time. Something must have motivated him to make the decision. This remains a mystery among academics.'

'Right.'

'The second mystery is about a poem he left behind.'

'A poem?'

'He left behind several poems. One of them is . . . *Kohi wabite kimi koso arame* . . .' In a loud, resonant voice, the old man recited a classical Japanese poem. He had no notes;

the piece had been committed to memory. Ayumi was captivated, though he couldn't understand the words.

'What do you think?' Samekawa asked. 'Gakuman is said to have written it, though it's not especially good.'

'It's not good?'

To Ayumi, all classical Japanese sounded poetic and elegant. He couldn't tell whether something was well written or not.

'It's not great,' Samekawa said. 'The feudal lord Uesugi Kenshin was quite knowledgeable about *waka*, or Japanese poetry, and his vassals studied it intently. Gakuman was born under Uesugi rule and had been exposed to *waka* from a very young age, but this poem seems to carry too much of the Heian influence from centuries before. It feels a bit anachronistic.'

'Is that . . . so.' Ayumi couldn't tell.

'This is a poem about love. And it is said to be based on a famous poem that Kenshin wrote as a young man. Kenshin's poem read: *For some this life may seem one of sacrifice / But praying to God is no different from longing after true love / Committed to God, this is where my heart belongs.*'

Ayumi vaguely remembered learning in a classical literature course about the *waka* technique of *honkatari*, in which a poet borrows a verse or two from a famous poem to give their own verse depth and background. Gakuman's poem, apparently, had been adapted from Kenshin's poem.

Samekawa continued. 'In his poem Gakuman expresses

a yearning for love, and his hope that the person in his heart will lead the life she wishes, without the suffering he has endured. Using Kenshin's poem as inspiration, he has replaced God with the person he holds dear.'

'Right.'

Samekawa looked at Ayumi with a serious expression.

'But here's the mystery. There is no woman in Gakuman's life for whom this poem could have been intended.'

'He wasn't married?'

'He did have a wife, but I don't believe he would have addressed her with such passion.' The old man shook his head. 'Gakuman had no children. Some have said that perhaps there was someone in his life with whom he had a secret relationship, or that the poem expressed his devotion to the emperor, or a teacher, or even a page. But none of those explanations sit right with me.'

'What do other academics have to say?'

The man screwed up his face.

'They say that it was written for his wife. While their relationship had evolved over the years, they say perhaps he was remembering when they first met.'

'Then . . .'

'But I have a different interpretation. Though the poem appears to have been written to a woman, my thinking is that it wasn't meant for any one person.'

79

Ayumi said nothing.

'A few other poems have been left behind in his hand-writing, but this is the only one about love. It doesn't make sense that he would write so passionately about love so late in his life. And then I realized, maybe he was writing to his villagers, and to the village itself.'

'The village itself?'

'Yes. The poem is proof that Gakuman was agonizing on behalf of his villagers, and though he fought not to show it, he was deeply conflicted by the choices he made. When I realized this, I felt as though I'd been struck by lightning.'

'OK...'

Ayumi didn't know what to make of the man's explanation, but didn't want to upset him. 'So it wasn't about romantic love.'

'Correct,' Samekawa nodded. 'My wish is to meet with Gakuman to clarify this.' He looked at Ayumi. 'If he says yes, I will bring all the knowledge that I have accumulated over the years. I will work on my classic Japanese so that I can communicate with him. If I am blessed with the opportunity to ask him myself, I will be so happy that I could die.'

Ayumi hadn't even finished a third of his dessert, while the old man's dish sat empty. He may not have been the world's most elegant eater, but the spoon he'd used lay resting on the plate, its end wrapped in the napkin the way it had come.

'I understand,' Ayumi nodded. Samekawa's face lit up. 'However, there is no guarantee that Mr Uekawa will accept. There is also the possibility that he has already met with someone—'

'Of course. Thank you. Thank you, you are a wonderful young man,' Samekawa jumped in before Ayumi could finish. He put his hands together in prayer pose.

Ayumi waved his hands. 'No, no, please.'

He promised Samekawa that he would be in touch, and they parted ways in front of the museum. The old man was taking the shinkansen back to Niigata tonight. Ayumi saw him off and released a small sigh, realizing only then that the man hadn't once mentioned payment.

Everybody he met usually asked about the fee. *Doesn't this cost money?* they worried. Or else they offered something as a token of their gratitude.

But the possibility of a fee never seemed to have crossed Samekawa's mind. Though if he was asked to pay, he would.

He didn't seem like a bad person, Ayumi thought as he watched the old man shrink into the distance. *But wow, is he strange.*

*

FOLLOWING HIS MEETING, Ayumi had planned to drop by the Akiyama house to see Anna.

The Akiyamas had managed the go-between long before his grandmother, and now he held the responsibility, and Ayumi continued to report every client request to the family; they still helped to make the hotel reservations.

When Ayumi arrived, Anna was lying on the floor watching TV in one of the large tatami-floored rooms. It looked like the superhero series that was popular with kids her age.

'You're here!' She sat up as Ayumi walked in, turning off the TV.

'I'm here.'

Anna and her parents welcomed Ayumi like family, even though he had moved out of the house that he'd lived in for years with his grandmother, his uncle – Ayumi's father's brother – and his family. He now lived alone in an apartment close to his office.

The house that Anna and her parents lived in belonged to Ayumi's great-uncle Sadayuki. His eldest son, Anna's grandfather, had previously lived in the house along with his wife and children, but as soon as Sadayuki appointed Anna as his successor, Anna's grandfather happily quit his work in the fortune-telling business and bought a house in the seaside town of Atami.

Tonight, Anna's parents were both away on business.

'You didn't go with them?' Ayumi asked.

'School,' she said bluntly. 'Unlike Mother and Father, I have *school*. It's compulsory, you know.'

'Right.'

He was sure she could have taken a day or two off to go with them, but the girl was a stickler about some things. She was ridiculously mature and bright, especially when compared to other kids her age, which came as no surprise to Ayumi. She was Sadayuki's great-grandchild, after all. Ayumi sometimes wondered if she had a fully grown human inside of her, someone who had lived several lives already. She possessed a wisdom that he felt was similar to Sadayuki and to his grandmother Aiko.

Even with Anna's parents away, the large Akiyama house with the traditional Japanese garden bustled with activity. There were housekeepers, butlers and other professional helpers to look after Anna. Almost as soon as Ayumi sat down, a piping hot cup of tea arrived in front of him.

'Thank you,' Anna said as a drink was set in front of her. She sounded like an adult, except that her drink was a soda with a straw, whereas Ayumi was served hot green tea and traditional *wagashi* sweets.

'So how was it? The request.'

'Well . . .'

As Ayumi filled her in, Anna's eyes shone. 'Wowwww!' she exclaimed. This was not her usual reaction.

'I don't know if this Uekawa-san is going to say yes, but I'll give it a try. There's a high likelihood he's already met with someone.'

'What happens in that case again?' Anna asked. 'Can you still try to negotiate with them?'

'No, the mirror doesn't light up.'

Negotiations with the deceased were done using a mirror that Ayumi had inherited from his grandmother. Under a moonlit sky, he placed his palm over the mirror and called the name of the deceased, who then appeared as a collection of light particles. Ayumi had yet to encounter a situation in which the summoned had already used up their one meeting, but his grandmother had informed him that in those instances, the mirror simply lay still.

'Huh.' Anna took a long sip of her soda and put her chin in her hands. 'I hope this Mr Samekawa gets his meeting. Seeing someone you've been studying your whole life . . . that's like getting to meet your idol.'

'Yeah.'

Anna was probably too young to be learning about the Feudal Era at school, and Ayumi didn't know how well versed she was in history.

'I just hope he's not disappointed,' she continued. 'He

said he'll be so happy he could *die*? Mr Samekawa probably knows this figure better than most people, but I hope he's not let down.'

'He sounds prepared for whatever disappointment might await him. I'm sure he's thought of every possible scenario,' Ayumi replied. But he also understood Anna's concern. Samekawa did seem to have a very high opinion of this figure; a good example being his interpretation of Gakuman's poem.

'But wait, how are you going to do this?' Anna asked.

'Do what?'

'The language.' She pointed to his dish of *wagashi* sweets. 'You gonna eat that?'

'Go ahead,' Ayumi replied.

'Yay!' Anna squealed, swiping his dish and putting her hands together. '*You* have to talk to this Uekawa person too, in order to negotiate. Oh, this reminds me of a case I heard about once. Someone wanted to be reunited with their dog.'

'Their *dog*?'

'Their dog. This was back when Great-Grandfather was still the go-between.'

Anna took a bite of the dessert and placed her forefinger on her chin as though deep in thought. 'He asked the owner why he wanted to see the dog and the owner replied, "Do I need a reason?" That's why Great-Grandfather decided to do it. Sometimes you don't have a reason. And then the owner said, "The go-between would be so much more powerful if you could give animals the ability to talk."'

'Wow.'

This person was wishing for a miracle on top of a pretty miraculous opportunity?

'Right?'

'So what happened?'

'It didn't work. The mirror didn't light up. Maybe meetings are only meant to happen between people.' She continued to chew. 'So what are you going to do? Since there's no translation option . . . what if you can't understand him? How are you going to communicate?'

'No worries there,' Ayumi said confidently, though the credit was not his. Anna threw him a dubious look, until she saw him pull an envelope out of his bag.

'Ohhh, a letter,' Anna said.

The old man had given it to Ayumi, asking him to use it in his negotiation. The envelope was addressed to Uekawa Gakuman in bold brush pen calligraphy. The letter itself was written on thick *washi* paper and folded like an accordion; a style of correspondence Ayumi had only seen in period dramas.

'Let me see,' Anna said, though she only stared at it once she had it in her hands. 'Thanks,' she said, holding the envelope out to Ayumi with both hands. 'He must really, really want this. I hope he gets to meet him.'

'Yeah,' Ayumi nodded. As he placed the letter back in his bag, his eyes landed on the sample toy he was working on. 'Oh yeah,' he said. 'I designed a toy that might become a product. It's a turtle, and I'm trying to decide on the colour. Want to see?'

The toy turtle, which was currently in production at Torino Workshop, moved forward and backward, making a sound when the feet moved. They were testing out the turtle shell in red, blue and yellow. Before he could take it out, Anna said, 'Green.'

Ayumi didn't have green. Anna grinned. 'If you don't know what colour to make a turtle shell, then green.'

'We don't have green.'

'Well, you should. No kid's gonna want some unrealistic colour like red or blue for a turtle.' She grabbed the toy from Ayumi's hand. 'Hey, this is pretty cute.' She flapped its feet and flashed a grin, looking like a child her age.

A FEW DAYS later, Ayumi finished a work meeting and took a break to call Samekawa with an update.

The old man picked up on the first ring. Ayumi could

almost hear him sitting up straight as he asked, 'How did it go?'

'He says he will see you,' Ayumi said. He heard Samekawa gulp. Relieved to be able to share the good news, Ayumi continued in an official tone, 'As for the meeting date . . .'

'Great. This is great. I'm in a meeting with the local museum as we speak, to figure out my guide schedule. They suggested I only come in on weekends when there are more visitors, but I said . . .'

Ayumi could tell from the restlessness on the other end that the joy and shock seemed to have hit Samekawa at once. He heard the rustling of papers and a sharp inhale. 'Um . . .'

'Yes?'

'Was Uekawa Gakuman . . . able to read my letter?'

'Yes, he was.'

The person who materialized as a faint collection of light particles atop the mirror's surface appeared old and frail. Clad in a plain brown kimono, he looked nothing like the Feudal Era lord Ayumi had been expecting.

'Hello,' Ayumi said nervously in contemporary Japanese.

Uekawa Gakuman stared straight into his eyes, which both intimidated him and made him wonder if the man understood. 'I have a letter for you,' he said, passing the man the envelope.

This was the first time Ayumi had ever handed a phys-ical item to the deceased during a negotiation, when they were a collection of light particles. He held his breath as Gakuman accepted the letter. He read it silently, and then he nodded slowly.

'Does that mean you accept?'

The man nodded again and made an *Mm* sound. Ayumi took that as a yes.

Hearing that his letter had been read, Samekawa let out a noise that came out like a moan. He sounded choked up.

Ayumi waited for him to catch his breath, and finally he heard, 'Thank you.'

'Of course.'

'Thank you. Thank you,' Samekawa sniffled. A moment later, he said, 'So where do I need to go, and when?'

KOHEI SAMEKAWA WAS not a dense man.

On his way to the most important meeting of his life, he stood in front of the shinkansen bathroom mirror and adjusted his bootlace tie. He'd had his thinning grey hair cut for the occasion, which he combed with care before putting on his hat.

When he retired from the high school where he'd long served as principal, he had used his retirement bonus to purchase a suit that would last the rest of his life. He brought it out of the closet today for the first time in ages.

Samekawa was not a dense man. He knew that this day would likely be the best day of his life.

Plain, serious, diligent, geek. The words used to describe him since childhood were not inaccurate. He always had his nose in a book, but he had no patience for subjects that didn't interest him. His love of history was so deep that he read every history book he could find, dissected ancient texts, learned all he could on the subject, even became a teacher so he could continue his academic studies. He realized, however, that not everybody understood him, nor did they care to. Students, the parents of students, even his colleagues. Everybody thought he was strange.

He knew that the students called him Sharkbrain because of the word *same*, or shark, in Samekawa. 'You know Sharkbrain's still single?' they gossiped. His being unmarried was apparently a marker that he was not normal. After his parents passed away and his siblings had married and left home, Samekawa was left with no close family. He knew that people thought he was weird and lonely.

He wasn't a dense man.

'He's a good principal, he's just weird,' his students said.

But Samekawa was never lonely. On the contrary, he saw himself as joyful and free. He didn't care what others thought.

When considering his own history and that of his hometown, Uekawa Gakuman always loomed large. Though he wasn't an academic with impressive credentials, Samekawa knew that nobody understood the life of the local hero, the region, the language, and the environment in which he lived, better than he did.

When he'd had the flash of inspiration that Gakuman's *waka* poem was not about romantic love, he felt a jolt that could only be described as fate. The realization was satisfaction enough, but then he learned about the go-between. He needed to know more. Frequenting libraries and museums to read everything he could find, he saw the go-between mentioned in mysterious folk tales about people meeting with the deceased. When he encountered a fellow volunteer guide who'd once made a request to the go-between, he thought it had to be destiny.

There was only one person in the world that Samekawa wished to see, a fact he found neither sad nor lonely. He was proud to have dedicated his entire life to that person.

Samekawa got off the shinkansen and transferred trains before finally arriving at Shinagawa Station.

He was not fond of crowds. After the age of eighty, he had been finding it increasingly strenuous to lift his feet, which used to take him everywhere. Even a few stairs now required him to catch his breath.

He took a gulp of air and regained his composure.

The lobby of the hotel where the meeting would be held dazzled so brightly that it nearly blinded him. He had never stayed in such glamorous accommodation before. But tonight was different. He had a room reserved under his name.

Arriving promptly at check-in time, he filled out the guest form at the front desk and noticed that his hand shook ever so slightly. He didn't want the clerk assuming that his age was to blame. *He* knew he was simply excited about meeting Uekawa Gakuman. He took a deep breath and patted his right hand gently with his left until the shaking stopped. He resumed filling out the form.

The bellhop carried his luggage up to his room, where he thought he might rest until seven o'clock, when he was to meet the go-between in the lobby. He closed his eyes, hoping to sleep off his fatigue from the long trip from Niigata. Finding it impossible to doze off, however, he got dressed and went downstairs. It was six o'clock.

When the young go-between stepped off the elevator, perhaps after preparing the room for the meeting, he appeared surprised to see Samekawa sitting in the lobby.

'Hello. I'm sorry, I didn't realize you'd arrived.'

'No, no. I thought I would stay here tonight. I have a room.'

The go-between widened his eyes. Samekawa laughed and said, 'This kind of event doesn't happen every day. I thought I would make the most of it.'

'Your meeting room is ready. You can see him now, if you wish.'

A tremendous thrill ran through the old man's body. 'Right.'

The meeting would last until morning. Once the sun rose, the deceased would disappear, and Samekawa was to come back down to the lobby. 'I understand. I'll remember not to go straight to my room after the meeting.'

'Yes, thank you,' the young man said with a smile.

The meeting would be held on the eleventh floor, two floors above Samekawa's room.

As the go-between handed him the card key, he remembered fumbling with his own room key earlier. He was glad to have practised beforehand.

The elevator arrived on the eleventh floor.

'Best of luck,' the go-between said.

Samekawa double-checked the room number and held his breath. He had prepared for this day, but the mix of nerves and excitement might leave him tongue-tied. He had brought sheets of paper and a calligraphy brush, just in case they needed to communicate through writing.

He knocked twice, not wanting to alarm anyone by ringing the doorbell. Even knocking might be a foreign concept, as there were no doors back in Gakuman's day.

When there was no answer, he slowly pushed open the door. As he peeked through the crack, he saw a figure at the far end of the room. He could make out the sleeve of a brown, threadbare *kasuri* fabric kimono. A man was seated on a chair with his legs folded under him.

Uekawa Gakuman.

SHORTLY BEFORE SIX the next morning, the old man came down to the lobby.

Ayumi saw him approaching and stood up quickly from his work, which he had laid out in front of him. The morning sun was streaming into the lobby. The meeting had continued the entire night, for as long as it could. He stuffed his papers into his bag and hurried across the lobby. 'Mr Samekawa!'

The man turned. 'Ah.'

Ayumi was taken slightly aback by his expression. The man looked as though he were still in a dream. The rims of his eyes were red, his cheeks flushed. Ayumi worried that the all-nighter might have been too hard on him, but Samekawa said, 'Hello, hello.' His voice sounded strong. Seeing him wobble slightly, Ayumi rushed over and led him to an empty sofa nearby.

'Ahhhh,' Samekawa sighed as he nestled back into the sofa. He then folded both arms across his face and leaned into them.

'Do you feel all right?' Ayumi asked hesitantly.

'Yes,' the man replied from behind his arms. Ayumi could see that his ears had flushed bright red.

'It was . . . Uekawa . . . Gakuman.'

The man met Ayumi's eye for the first time since coming down to the lobby. 'It was really and truly him. No, if that was an impersonator, then I'm happy to be fooled. I'm happy to have exchanged words with him, to have heard his thoughts with these very ears.'

Ayumi was surprised the meeting had lasted as long as it had. Samekawa was elderly, and he was encountering Uekawa Gakuman, someone from an entirely different era. What could they have discussed?

Samekawa's eyes were bloodshot and bleary.

'May I get you some water?'

The old man shook his head. He seemed unable to contain his excitement.

'His words . . .'

'Yes.'

'He spoke in a thick local dialect, and his words and pronunciation were foreign to me. Our communication was frankly a mess. I'm glad I asked you to give him the letter beforehand. We were able to communicate somewhat through writing, gestures and a few spoken words here and there, but if we hadn't been from the same town, I doubt that I would have picked up on anything. I don't think that anyone could understand his dialect, no matter how brilliant an academic they might be.'

'Was he who you imagined he would be?'

Samekawa regarded Ayumi for a while, then nodded. 'I expected to meet with a younger Gakuman, but he appeared today as I imagine he looked near the end of his life. He wore a tattered kimono, just as I had read and heard. He was a man who helped his villagers plant rice, after all.'

'Right.'

'There is a portrait in our local museum that is said to be of Gakuman, but I know now that it bears no resemblance to him. Now that I've seen him, I feel strange having to introduce it to tourists.'

Ayumi didn't want to keep the old man too long, but Samekawa didn't seem to mind. If anything, he seemed eager to share his excitement with anyone who would listen.

'I'd envisioned him as this noble figure, but today I learned he may have had a great sense of humour. I asked if he didn't mind my requesting a meeting with him, but he seemed to be enjoying himself.'

'Enjoying himself?'

'He said he was curious to see what kind of oddball would want to meet with him,' the old man laughed. 'He also said that the idea of meeting with the deceased wasn't inconceivable. In fact, he might have heard something along those lines before. He seemed to have many questions for me. From the clothes I wore, to the view from the hotel room. He asked what era this was, what kind of society we lived in, who now governs the land. I didn't think I would ever make it out of there,' Samekawa said, sounding almost gleeful.

'Even as the sun started to rise, he continued asking questions until the last possible moment, about the current political system, about what had happened to his territory after his death. I worried that it would be distressing to learn we had fought with other countries, but he wanted to know every detail. He kept blinking in disbelief.' Samekawa's eyes welled up. 'It was an honour. To be the one to inform Uekawa Gakuman of our country's history after his passing.'

'And were you able to have your questions answered?'

'Yes,' the man said smoothly. 'He said he didn't give it much thought.'

'I'm sorry?'

'The reason behind his heroic decision to keep his villagers at home,' Samekawa said. 'He said he was simply afraid to send them, and he was worried that no one would be left to tend to the farms. That's why he said no. But he also said that if he was ordered by the Uesugi clan once more, he might have changed his mind and answered yes. It was only because Uesugi Kenshin was nearly unbeatable in battle and he almost always returned victorious that he didn't need more men.'

Ayumi stared.

So Uekawa Gakuman hadn't been a hero after all. As though he had read Ayumi's mind, the old man laughed.

'Even from the way he spoke, I sensed he must have been a rather indecisive leader. Down-to-earth and personable, yes. But not authoritative. Decisions were made for him while he pondered whether to go this way or that. He did seem to have luck on his side. And in that way, perhaps he was a savvy leader.'

'And about the *waka* poem . . .'

'Oh, that's a funny story too. Uekawa Gakuman didn't write that.'

'*What?*' Ayumi cried. But Samekawa didn't appear at all let down.

He laughed. 'He didn't write it, but the episode speaks

volumes about what kind of man he was. It turns out that he penned the poem on behalf of a vassal who couldn't read or write.'

'Like a ghostwriter?'

The old man nodded happily. 'Which explains why the poem doesn't sound like something he would write. During peaceful times, people often gathered in the village to read their poems aloud. One day, a young vassal came to Gakuman and said that he wished to participate, but because he was illiterate, Gakuman sat down with him and adapted one of Uesugi Kenshin's famous poems into a new verse, which he then wrote down. When I first brought this up with him, he had no memory of it. But he gradually remembered as he recounted the story.'

'I see,' Ayumi said, feeling a wave of disappointment. He could glean from the stories that Gakuman had been a kind man, but was that what Samekawa had hoped for?

'Um . . .'

'Yes?'

'Weren't you . . . disappointed?'

The old man had been so eager to meet his hero. Surprisingly, he nodded. 'Of course I was. Learning there was so little meaning behind his big decision. He wasn't a hero after all, nor was he a poet. But isn't that what history is all about? History is whatever people wish and choose to believe happened. To know that I am the only living human who knows the truth about Gakuman, however? Now *that* fills me with a different kind of emotion.'

Ayumi could imagine his satisfaction.

Samekawa stared off into the distance. 'He looked as though . . . he wasn't finished. After I had answers to both of my questions, he started to . . . I don't know . . . squirm.'

The word 'squirm' sounded so strange coming out of the old man's mouth, Ayumi couldn't help but smile. Samekawa licked his lips. 'He asked me whether his life was worthy of my devotion. Whether people remembered his name after his death.'

Samekawa fell silent, amplifying the quiet of the early morning lobby. As Ayumi watched, the old man turned away and looked out into the distance again. His eyes reddened again and began to waver.

'He thanked me. Said he never imagined that his life would be of any worth to anyone.' When he regarded Ayumi again, his eyes once again shone brightly. 'Thank you,' he said. 'Thank you. Thank you. I cannot believe that I had Gakuman say those words to me.'

'I didn't do anything . . .'

For this old man, Uekawa Gakuman didn't need to be a hero.

'Thank you,' Samekawa said again.

Perhaps he was directing his gratitude, not to Ayumi, but to Uekawa Gakuman. To the figure who ended up being *more* than the historical figure he'd long admired.

AFTER ACCOMPANYING SAMEKAWA back to his hotel room, Ayumi walked to the station to board a train to Karuizawa.

It was always this way for him, bouncing between his go-between work and his day job. At least he would be able to nap for an hour or so on the bullet train.

He was relieved to know that he would not run into Samekawa on the shinkansen platform. He hoped the man was sleeping soundly in his room. Either that, or he was too excited to sleep. Either way, he imagined it must be a good morning for him.

On their way back to his hotel room, Samekawa had said, 'It never once crossed my mind in my seventies.'

'I'm sorry?'

'The meaning of one's life. That sort of thing.'

He seemed unconcerned about whether Ayumi was following.

'But once I passed the age of eighty, I started to think about it more. In the context of the go-between, thinking not so much about who *I* want to see, but more about whether anyone would want to see *me* after I'm gone. I understood where Gakuman was coming from. Though I have no expectations myself.'

His tone was light and free of self-pity.

Not knowing what else to say, Ayumi said, 'I had no idea you were over eighty.'

'I am.'

'I never would have guessed it.'

'I get that often,' Samekawa laughed. The morning light came in from the hallway window, adding a glow to his face. 'Thank you for today. It was easily the best day of my life.'

Did my life have meaning? Will I be remembered after my death?

Those were questions Ayumi had never considered. He understood Samekawa's words but couldn't yet feel them in his bones.

As he made his way up the path to the studio, his work phone pinged. It was a message from Nao of Torino Workshop. He had called her at the start of the week, and she had sprung quickly into action.

Her message read, *I agree it should definitely be green!*

Attached to the message was a photo of the toy turtle

with a green shell. Instantly more endearing. Ayumi's steps felt lighter as he walked.

Is this what Mr Samekawa was talking about? The meaning of one's life. One's history. One's name. Compared to the two elderly men, what he'd created was tiny, trivial really. But it thrilled him. Something he had designed was coming to life.

Kids will love this! he texted back, though he would be seeing Nao in a few minutes.

3

The Rule of the Mother

KEEP HAVING THE dream, over and over, that I'm sinking in water.

For some reason, I don't dream about what actually happened. Last night, for example, it went something like this.

We've driven out to a town by the sea somewhere – me, my husband and our daughter Mei. My husband steers the car into what appears to be a parking structure built in the ocean. The steel-frame parking structure, which is full of cars, has large gaps in the footing from where you can see the dark water beneath. The gaps seem big enough for a person to fall through.

I am fraught with anxiety.

Strangely, my worry isn't about finding a parking spot or falling into the water, car and all. I'm more concerned that my husband will say, 'You want me to park here? It's too dangerous.' As predicted, in the dream, he remarks, 'This is bad. Why don't the two of you get out and wait while I park?'

I think irritably that if it was truly dangerous, they wouldn't have built the structure here in the first place, but I keep my mouth shut. I undo Mei's car seat and lift her into my arms. We get out of the car, though I doubt this will affect his ability to park.

The water appears to be rising beneath our feet, the waves amplifying. The ocean looks deep. I think about the bad weather we had yesterday. It would be horrible to fall in, I think, as I look down at Mei. What if *she* falls in? My mind plays back the drowning accidents I've seen on the news. I think about the parents who dived in after their children and ended up losing their own lives. I can hear the news anchors' voices now, warning parents not to go in after their children.

I have to warn Mei. Tell her to be careful. But I don't. She'll be all right, I think. She'll never fall in. I watch as she gazes curiously at the water.

And that's when it happens. Mei falls through a crack and plunges into the sea. She seems to have fallen, not by accident, but out of curiosity. As if she wanted to know what it would feel like to fall.

In my dream, I scream. I dive in after Mei, through the

same gap where she'd just slipped. I learn that the warning on the news about not going after your child is ridiculous.

Why didn't I tell her to be careful? I should have warned her.

No, I can still save her. She has to be saved.

The two thoughts collide in my head.

Underwater, it is dark but clear. I see Mei's back, which would soon be carrying a brand-new *randoseru* backpack that all elementary school children take to school. I see her clearly, as though I'm peering through swimming goggles. In reality, nothing would be visible underwater.

I reach for her, frantically trying to close the gap between us, but my body doesn't move as fast as I need it to. Mei isn't fighting. She simply sinks, as if she has already lost consciousness.

I realize that I can't save her. Mei is sinking. Who knows how much deeper she has to go. I won't make it in time. I can't reach her.

Mei! I scream inside.

Even in my dream, I know that I can still make it back up to the water's surface. If I let my daughter go. But how do I abandon her when I can still *see* her?

I'm going to die with Mei. I'm going to die with her because I couldn't keep her from falling in.

My husband will get out of the car and dive in after us.

Before long, he will realize he is powerless. And he too will die. That's what will happen, and I can't do anything to stop it.

We're all going to die. This is how death arrives. There is no way I will lose Mei and continue living myself.

I don't regret this.

In my dream, that's what I believe.

AYUMI SHIBUYA SAT in the hotel lounge in Shinagawa, listening quietly.

Across from him were Shoichi and Misato Shigeta, a couple in their thirties who wished to see their daughter Mei, whom they lost in a drowning accident five years ago. Ayumi had never had a husband and wife come to him together before. They knew, without him having to explain, that only one of them would be able to meet with the deceased.

'I'm hoping Mei's mother can see her,' Shoichi said.

His wife began describing, without emotion, the dreams she'd been having since losing their daughter.

'The dreams are nothing like what happened in real life. In reality, I didn't dive in after her. W-we didn't even know she'd disappeared. Neither my husband nor I . . . were watching her.'

Ayumi nodded. They didn't need for him to say anything. The couple had brought a photograph showing a smiling family of three, standing in front of a jetty somewhere. The parents looked bright-eyed and youthful, unrecognizable from the couple who sat before him now. They each held their daughter's hand.

Mei was six at the time. She would be starting elementary school the following year. Her cute face, little hands. Red check-patterned dungarees.

'This was taken the day she died.'

Ayumi looked at the dark ocean behind the family, above which heavy clouds hung.

Today's meeting felt longer and heavier than usual. He was used to receiving requests from people wanting to reconnect with a family member. But he would never grow accustomed to the devastation of parents who wished to see a child they'd lost.

Shoichi Shigeta's voice had been trembling on the phone.

'We don't feel that we deserve a meeting, but can we share our story with you?'

The Shigetas had been visiting a beach in Chiba that day. Shoichi and Misato were fishing from the jetty, and their daughter had been enthralled by the caught fish in the bucket. 'Fishies!' she exclaimed.

'We were careless,' Shoichi started, looking at Ayumi

across the table. He spoke slowly and deliberately, detailing the day, though it must have been excruciating to recount.

The couple had sat side-by-side on the concrete jetty with their rods, immersed in their fishing, when they realized their daughter was nowhere to be seen. They scrambled to their car to see if she was hiding behind it, scanning their surroundings frantically.

'My wife and I don't remember hearing a splash. We looked everywhere. When we realized she was really gone, we called the police. But even after the Coast Guard were deployed, we were sure she wasn't in the ocean.'

While her husband explained, Misato stared vacantly out of the window. The afternoon sunshine glided across the lush green grass of the courtyard.

'We can't remember ever hearing a splash, but we panicked and looked at the water, of course. We should have dived in immediately, but we were more worried that something might have happened to her on land, that she may have been kidnapped. I can't explain why we thought that. We just did.'

'Right,' Ayumi finally said. Misato looked at him, her eyes coming into focus for a moment.

'They found Mei that night,' she said. 'She'd apparently fallen in when neither of us were looking. They pulled her dead body out of the water.'

She seemed to be punishing herself by saying the words out loud: *dead body.*

'Her death was declared an accident. And we knew the police were right. Children can and will just disappear like that, without making a sound.'

Ayumi could tell that it had taken years for them to arrive at a point where they could talk about the incident. The long silence that filled the room seemed to signal that.

When Misato finally lifted her face, she said, 'Mei kept demonstrating to us how she could balance on the jetty. I saw her peer into the ocean several times, and each time I thought, I have to tell her to be careful. But she hadn't got herself into trouble so far, and I didn't say anything. We'd been to this jetty many times before, and even if she did happen to fall in, we thought we'd be able to jump in and save her.'

Shoichi turned to Ayumi. 'We're hoping you can help us see our daughter,' he said. 'We learned about the go-between at a gathering for parents who had lost their children. We were told there might be a way to see our child again.'

Ayumi wondered if any of those people had seen the go-between themselves. The Shigetas didn't say. But something about the parents' stories must have convinced them the go-between was real.

Shoichi continued. 'Forgive me for saying this, but we

didn't believe it at first. We were being bombarded by creepy offers at the time, from religious organizations and people telling us they could help us get over our loss. I don't know how they even found us.'

'Right.'

'It took us five years to finally be able to say, OK, let's give it a try. Part of it was doubt. But I think the bigger reason is that we didn't think we deserved a meeting. Our carelessness had killed our child.'

The word 'killed' echoed sharply in the afternoon lounge. Shoichi, who had been speaking steadily up to that point, took in a short breath. His eyes reddened. 'And we didn't know if she . . .' Next to him, Misato's eyes also welled. 'We didn't know if she would want to see us. That's what we were afraid of. What we're still afraid of.'

I'm sure that won't be the case, Ayumi started to say, but stopped. These people had suffered for years. He could feel the weight of their regret, and nothing he said could help to alleviate that.

They looked at Ayumi and lowered their heads.

'We would be grateful for your help.'

They spoke to him respectfully, although he was many years younger than them.

Ayumi had heard of families falling apart after losing their children to accidents, and though the Shigetas appeared supportive of one another, his guess was that it hadn't always been this way.

'I understand,' Ayumi replied. 'I'll do my best.'

WHETHER SOMEONE CAN *find their way to the go-between is determined by fate.*

Alone in the hotel lounge following the meeting with the Shigetas, Ayumi thought about his grandmother's words.

Some people try numerous times and can't get through, while others, the people who really need it, somehow find their way.

A few of the meetings Ayumi had experienced in his early days as the go-between seemed to confirm this. There was a reason to reunite. But a few times, he was left wondering if people were better off not reconnecting at all.

Did his meeting with the Shigetas feel especially fraught because they had not yet come to terms with their daughter's death? Of course there was no perfect 'resolution' in the death of a loved one, but many who came to him had managed to work out their feelings, even as they continued to grieve. Maybe a path to the go-between had opened up to them *because* they had reached that stage. But the couple he met today didn't appear close to that emotional stage at all. There must be a reason, then, that they had found him. He hoped that there was.

He looked at his watch and saw that he had ten minutes to spare until his next meeting. After that, he was scheduled to see a client for his toy-design day job and then he would finally be able to return to the office at night. Though he normally tried to schedule go-between meetings on separate days, with this being a hectic month, he had no choice but to fit them both in today.

He thought about squeezing in some work for ten minutes but decided it would be unprofessional to have his work papers scattered about when the next person arrived. Anna would not be happy. He took a sip of water from his last meeting and glanced at the lounge entrance, where he noticed an elegant woman who looked to be in her seventies. She wore a floral blouse, shimmering black trousers and stylish tinted glasses.

Must be Tokiko Ogasawara, the person he was scheduled to meet next. She'd said on the phone that she was seventy-four, though she looked much younger. A waiter approached the woman, who said thank you but declined his help. She headed straight over to Ayumi.

'Pardon me, are you the go-between?' she asked in a clear, vibrant voice.

Ayumi nodded. 'Yes. Hello. It's nice to meet you.'

Go-between requests usually came in about once a month, but some months he received two or three calls. When this happened, he often scheduled multiple meetings on the same night – the night of the full moon – for that was when they could last the longest. Three was the maximum number of meetings he'd scheduled in a night, and though he worried about having to turn clients away if he received more than that, he'd strangely not run into that dilemma yet.

When two or more meet-ups were scheduled for the same night, he made sure to stagger the times so the clients wouldn't run into each other. And while he never specified when they should finish, the meetings seemed to come to a natural end at varying times, never simultaneously. Maybe that was predestined too, like his grandmother had said.

'Please, have a seat,' Ayumi said as he prepared himself mentally for the second request of the day.

'I WISH TO see my daughter.'

Hearing the words come out of the woman's mouth, Ayumi thought of the Shigetas and inhaled sharply. Tokiko's expression was not one of despair, however. She continued to wear the same gentle smile as when she first arrived.

'Your daughter.'

'Yes. She passed away over twenty years ago. From breast cancer, when she was twenty-six. The doctors at Hibiya Hospital did everything they could, but the cancer spread quickly because she was so young.'

When taking a request, Ayumi normally asked for the name of the deceased, the date they died and the reason for the meeting. Nothing more. The woman gave him more detail than he needed, but he listened as she spoke openly and honestly.

'This is Eiko. When she was healthy,' Tokiko said, placing a sepia-toned photograph on the table. She must have carried it with her at all times.

In the photo a young woman smiled luminously, her hair cascading in large, full waves. A tall, broad-shouldered man stood by her side with his arms wrapped around her. He was not Japanese. The two looked as though nothing could get in the way of their joy.

'That's Karl, my daughter's husband,' Tokiko said. 'He's German. They got married nine months before she died. Eiko's full name is Eiko Birkner.'

'She was married to a German man?'

'Yes. It's nothing unusual now, but back then, I would say it was still quite uncommon. We were shocked when she came to us and said that she wanted to marry someone who wasn't Japanese,' Tokiko said and laughed. 'Eiko studied abroad during college. She majored in children's literature, and she stayed in Germany after graduation to continue her research. We weren't a wealthy family, but we'd been saving for our two daughters since they were children, for when they got married. We used the money we'd saved for Eiko to pay for her time abroad.' Tokiko reminisced fondly, pushing her glasses up. 'I was a regular housewife and had never worked, and while I don't regret getting married, if someone asked whether I'd done everything I wanted to do in my life, I don't know that I would have an answer. So I told myself that if my daughters ever found something they were passionate about, I would support them.'

'That's great,' Ayumi said, and meant it.

'Thank you,' Tokiko nodded happily. 'Not a lot of people were given the opportunity to study abroad back then, and I think I felt some pride in my daughter taking that big step. We sent her off saying that we could pay for college but that she needed to pay her own way after graduation.'

'Right.'

'I think it was about five years after she moved to Germany.' Tokiko took a sip of her coffee. 'Eiko came home for the New Year holiday and said she wanted to introduce us to someone. My husband and I assumed she had met a Japanese man overseas, so when she said his name was Karl, my goodness, we were speechless!' Tokiko said in a light, playful tone, and Ayumi couldn't help but smile.

'And did you meet him?'

'We didn't. My husband and I were dead set against the idea, saying that nothing good could come out of two people from different cultures coming together. We told her that we didn't approve, that we didn't send her abroad for this. We urged her to give up the idea and come home.'

'And your daughter . . .'

'She agreed. She said that she wouldn't marry Karl without our blessing.' Tokiko paused, looking sombre for the first time. 'I know we did a terrible thing. Here was our daughter, a strong girl who could do whatever she put her mind to, putting our needs before hers.'

'Right.'

'So Eiko went back to Germany and continued her research. A while later, we got a call. She said, "Mom, I'm sick. They say it's breast cancer. Can I come back to Japan for treatments?"' Tokiko spoke without emotion, which was probably how her daughter had sounded on the phone over twenty years ago. 'When she came back to Japan, Karl was with her. He'd come all this way to support her, and gradually, our thinking about him, and the two of them together, began to shift. After we finally gave them our blessing, they held a wedding in Japan, with Karl wearing a *hakama* and everything.'

'Wow.'

'My daughter died less than a year later. But they both said that they couldn't have been happier for the time they had.' Tokiko gazed out at the lawn, which sparkled under the sun. 'After Eiko passed, Karl said to us, "I would like to take the two of you to Germany, to see where she lived." I'd never set foot outside of Japan, and I was anxious about going without Eiko, but Hiroko – that's Eiko's younger sister – gave me the push I needed. She said that if there was even a small part of me that was interested, then I had to go.'

'Right.'

'My decision to contact the go-between was also something I discussed with Hiroko and her husband, by the way. I live with them now, after my husband died two years ago.' Tokiko took another sip of coffee. 'They were shocked to hear that somebody could set up meetings with the deceased and said it had to be a scam. But again, they said if this is something I really want to do, I should give it a try.'

'Were they worried?'

'They were, but in the end, they left the decision to me. Do it at your own risk, they said. They did warn me that if I was asked to pay an astronomical fee, I was to walk out of the meeting. But you're saying that isn't necessary?'

'That's right.'

Tokiko had enquired about the fee in her initial phone

call. 'I don't mind paying if it's within reason,' she had said, to which Ayumi had replied, 'No, no, no, no.'

'I told them that a young man answered when I called, and that he sounded quite handsome. They were surprised by that too.'

'Uh, no, um . . .' Ayumi stammered, which made Tokiko laugh.

'When I asked Hiroko if she wanted to come with me today, she gave me a look and said, "Why, Mom – are you scared to go alone?" She had to work and couldn't come anyway, but I know she trusts me.'

Her daughter may not believe in the go-between, but she believes in her mother, Ayumi thought. He felt their bond and got a sense of the kind of daughter Eiko had been as well.

'Oops, I've gone off on a tangent,' Tokiko said, readjusting her seat. 'Karl isn't fluent in Japanese, but the trip to Germany was wonderful. He introduced us to Eiko's friends, many of whom said, "We've been wanting to meet you!" I asked if they'd heard about us, and they all said, "Of course! You're the reason Eiko was able to come to this country at all. We would never have met her if it hadn't been for you." Karl had invited us knowing that her friends wanted to meet us.'

Tokiko looked at Ayumi. 'I want to thank my daughter. My opinions were not always correct, and my daughter helped to broaden my thinking.' She took a deep breath. 'I wish I'd been able to give her a stronger, healthier body, one that wouldn't give out on her. If she didn't have me for a mother, she might have had a more fulfilling life.'

Seeing Ayumi's surprised expression, Tokiko asked, 'Are you all right?'

'Oh, I'm . . . don't mind me.'

The elderly woman gave a soft laugh and said, 'I'm so grateful for this opportunity. Thank you, Mr Go-Between.' She bowed her head.

'I'll do everything I can,' Ayumi said.

THE LITTLE GIRL who had died, Mei Shigeta, was younger than Anna.

As he drove to the Akiyama house, where he had been invited to dinner, Ayumi thought about the photo her parents had shown him. Now that there was a small child in his own life, incidents involving young children hit closer to home.

Anna's parents were home tonight. 'Hey, Ayumi!' her father boomed as he walked into the house.

'Anna! Time to turn off the TV! You promised only thirty minutes. You need to do your homework!' Anna's mother's voice echoed through the hall.

'It's only been twenty minutes!' Anna hollered back.

'It has not!' her mother's voice grew louder.

While Anna may be the 'head of the Akiyama house', she was also an eight-year-old child.

'Come on, you two! Ayumi's here!' Anna's father yelled. 'Sorry. It's so loud in this house.' His smile reminded Ayumi of his great-uncle Sadayuki. Anna's father was Sadayuki's grandson, which meant Ayumi and Anna's father were second cousins – though there was an age gap between them. Ayumi called Anna's parents 'Aunt' and 'Uncle', though technically, they were his cousins. No term existed to describe Ayumi's relation to Anna.

'No problem,' he replied, taking off his shoes and stepping into the spacious house that always smelled of fresh tatami.

'Heyyy, Ayumi! Hard day?' Anna came out of the back, not sounding at all like an eight-year-old.

'It was fine,' Ayumi replied like he would to an adult.

He could smell miso soup cooking in the kitchen and wondered if his childhood house had been this way too. He remembered very little about his parents, who had both died when he was a young boy.

After dinner, Ayumi joined Anna's mother at the sink to wash the dishes. He appreciated that she let him help rather than treat him as a guest.

There were many housekeepers to do the cooking and cleaning, but when Anna's mother was home, she made it a point to cook their meals.

Ayumi washed and rinsed the dishes, while his aunt dried. Watching her hold Anna's small rice bowl with a rabbit illustration, he found himself asking, 'Do a lot of mothers think that everything that happens to their child is their responsibility?'

His aunt looked at him quizzically.

'It's just . . . someone I met today as the go-between said something like that.'

'I see.'

He couldn't stop thinking about Tokiko Ogasawara's comment about wishing she could have given her daughter a stronger body. Ayumi could see how a parent who had lost their child in an accident, crime, or even suicide, might feel partly responsible for the death. But do parents blame themselves when their child dies from illness?

Tokiko had supported her daughter's wish to go abroad and to marry the man she loved, receiving gratitude from her daughter *and* her daughter's friends. And still, she thought, *If only she'd had a different mother.*

'The person I met today . . . she struck me as a really good mother. She was supportive of her daughter and helped her achieve her dreams. And her daughter was grateful. But the woman blamed herself for not being able to give her a strong, healthy body.'

'That's how a parent thinks. Not a day goes by where we don't feel responsible for our child,' his aunt smiled wanly.

'Even you?'

'Of course. When Anna doesn't listen, or she doesn't clean up after herself, I feel like I haven't done my job. When she doesn't turn off the TV and she throws her clothes on the floor without folding them, I think it's because I'm away so much and can't always be with her.'

'Hey, are you talking about me?' Anna called from the next room, over the sound of the TV she was supposedly watching.

'No!' her mother called back. She then smiled at Ayumi. 'Your mother was that way too. When you were little, she worried that it was her fault you couldn't eat bell peppers and onions.'

'My mom?' He hadn't expected to be brought into the conversation. 'Did you ever talk to her about things like that?'

'Mm. When I was engaged to your uncle and was beginning to spend more time with people in this family. Can you eat them now? Bell peppers and onions?' she teased.

'Yeah. When I was in elementary school and couldn't do a pullover on the bars, Grandma tricked me and said, "You'll be able to do it if you eat bell peppers." Onions too, even though I don't remember the story behind that one.'

'Ha! That does sound like Auntie Aiko,' his aunt cackled. 'Your mother was a whiz in the kitchen, but even she thought it was her fault you couldn't eat peppers and onions. Or maybe she *wanted* to believe she was the reason.'

'Why?'

'Because parents want their kids to be kids forever. Even when the child no longer wants to be babied. I suppose you could call it a mother's ego.'

His aunt took a clean plate from Ayumi and dried it. 'Is the request from a mother wishing to see her child?' she asked with gentleness in her voice.

'Yeah.'

'That's hard.'

His aunt's expression clouded over without him having to fill her in on the details. He finished washing the dishes and turned off the faucet.

It *was* hard. Both requests.

The negotiations proceeded smoothly under a moonlit sky, and he walked away with two yeses.

Ayumi had started with Eiko because he needed a bit more time to prepare, mentally and emotionally, to meet with young Mei. When Eiko learned her mother had requested her, she looked surprised but delighted.

When he summoned the little girl, she appeared wearing the same check dungarees as in the photo. Standing in the bright light of the mirror, she stared at Ayumi with a confused expression. She then looked shyly around in search of someone.

'Mei Shigeta,' Ayumi called out, to which Mei perked up, raised her hand and yelled, 'Here!' Ayumi jumped. This was probably how she answered to her preschool teacher during roll call.

'Do you want to see your mom?'

She went quiet, as though she didn't how to answer. She folded her hands behind her and after a pause, she nodded.

THE NIGHT OF the next full moon was forecast to be clear.

On days when he was to fulfil his role as go-between, Ayumi found that his own emotions were all over the place. The go-between was a witness, not a participant, but he couldn't help but be affected by his clients' states of mind. Some meetings he looked forward to, and others he found himself dreading.

Tonight's meetings would take place in separate rooms of the same hotel in which he had met the clients. The Shigetas were scheduled to arrive at six-thirty, Tokiko at six forty-five.

Earlier that day, he had been in Nagano Prefecture visiting Torino Workshop to discuss the turtle toy they were collaborating on. The toy was in its final production stages and would soon hit store shelves.

'Oh, hey, Ayumi. The toy's done. Just a sec,' said Taisho, the owner of the studio, who came out of the back with a hand towel wrapped around his head. 'Hey, Ayumi's here!' he called out to the back of the studio.

'Hello,' Ayumi said, moved by the warm welcome.

'Hi, Shibuya-san!' Nao greeted him as she emerged wearing a work apron.

Ayumi didn't have a family. After losing both of his parents as a young boy, he lived with his grandmother and his uncle's family, until his grandmother passed away when he was in college. Once Ayumi graduated and got a job, he moved out of his uncle's house, though he still visited frequently and was always welcomed home. He loved the family dearly, yet he'd felt deep down that their house was not his.

His grandmother was perhaps the only person he could genuinely call family. When the time finally came for him to say farewell to her, Ayumi felt he'd been given time to prepare. There may come a day in the future when he might want to see her again, but for the time being, he thought he was doing all right.

It was only in the past few years that he started to think of his own family whenever a client requested a family member. He'd never made the connection before.

After his meeting with Taisho and Okusan, he noticed that he hadn't seen Nao since he first arrived. She took care of accounting and administrative tasks at the workshop, and there was nothing unusual about her not sitting in on their meeting. But she had joined them before, bouncing ideas back and forth with Ayumi.

'Thank you again for everything. Um, is Nao around today?' he asked, packing up his bag.

'Yeah, she's uh . . . tied up,' Taisho said apologetically.

Ayumi sensed his hesitation and decided not to pursue it. He said goodbye and started on his way towards the bus stop, when he heard from the studio, 'You need to let it go.'

Ayumi didn't mean to listen in, but he stopped and turned to see Nao and Taisho through the window. They didn't look like their usual selves. A few wooden toys lay on the table, and Nao was gripping one of the pieces. When she lifted her face, she was biting her lip, and her eyes had lost their usual sparkle. She said something to her father, but Ayumi felt he needed to leave before he found out what it was.

He'd seen something he shouldn't have.

*

THE SHIGETAS ARRIVED together in the hotel lobby.

Misato stepped towards Ayumi and gave a small bow. 'Thank you for arranging this.'

Her husband said he would wait in the lobby. 'Is that all right?' he asked.

'Of course,' Ayumi replied. He handed Misato the room key and was about to lead her to the elevator when he noticed something on her bag. He didn't say anything.

'See you in a bit,' Shoichi said.

'I'll see you,' his wife replied, then flipped the keychain hanging on the outside of her bag to the inside, making it less visible.

Her daughter was waiting in Room 805.

Ayumi had been reluctant to leave the little girl alone in the room earlier, even if he was going downstairs to greet her mother. 'I'm going to get your mom, OK?' He wanted to bring Misato up as quickly as possible.

'Your daughter is waiting for you,' he said as the elevator reached the eighth floor.

'Thank you,' Misato replied, her lips quivering.

Tokiko Ogasawara arrived in the hotel lobby minutes later.

She wore a modern-looking blouse with a different pattern from last time, and her hair appeared shorter. 'I got it done,' she smiled.

Shoichi Shigeta was nowhere to be seen. There was no rule stating that clients couldn't speak with one another, but Ayumi was relieved that their paths wouldn't be crossing.

Tokiko was as talkative as ever today.

'My daughter is coming around dawn tomorrow to pick me up. I told her I could get home by myself, but she insisted. I hope that's OK.'

'Of course. I'm glad someone will be meeting you here.'

He sensed the lobby would be busier than usual tomorrow morning.

Tokiko's daughter was waiting in Room 1603. Ayumi handed the elderly woman the key and led her to the elevator.

'I'm nervous,' she said as they stepped in, more to herself than to him. 'I couldn't sleep last night.'

'Your daughter is looking forward to seeing you.'

They reached the sixteenth floor, and Ayumi saw Tokiko off from the elevator. He watched as she closed her eyes briefly in front of the hotel room, inserted her key, then slowly opened the door.

MISATO SHIGETA TOOK a deep breath.

She didn't dream about sinking last night. Maybe she'd been too worked up about the meeting the following day.

She'd fallen into a deep sleep almost as soon as she climbed into bed; she couldn't remember the last time that had happened.

She opened the door. As she entered, a small shadow turned towards her.

It was Mei. She wore the same red check dungarees as the day she passed away, and her hair was in pigtails. Her daughter was alive.

'Mei!' she called. The girl's face lit up.

'Mommy!' she yelled and ran into her mother's arms. Misato wrapped her daughter in a tight embrace. *So this is where you were.* She'd finally found her. Not a day went by when she didn't recall her daughter's pale cheeks and colourless lips as they pulled her out of the water. Here was her little girl now, warm and wide-eyed.

'I'm sorry,' she croaked. She didn't know how much Mei understood about what had happened. Did she know what death was? Not wanting to scare her, Misato had told herself not to apologize or mention the accident. But she couldn't help it.

'I'm so sorry, Mei. Mommy wasn't looking. I'm so sorry. I miss you so much.'

She squeezed her daughter tightly, but Mei squirmed as she always did when Misato held her for too long. 'That's too tight, Mommy!'

'I'm sorry,' Misato repeated, laughing. But she didn't want to let her go. 'Can I hold you just a bit longer?'

Wiping the tears that streamed down her face, she looked at Mei, who only stared back quizzically.

TOKIKO OGASAWARA CLOSED her eyes before opening the door.

She placed a hand on her chest and felt her heart racing. Will she get it right? Suddenly, she was frightened. *You went over this so many times. You'll be fine.* She opened her eyes and inserted the card key in the slot.

Somebody stood at the far end of the room. *Oh.* It was Eiko, young and healthy, wearing her favourite dress. Her hair – not the wig she wore after she lost her hair – was curled just the way she liked.

Eiko covered her mouth in surprise. 'Mom?' Her voice was so bright.

Twenty years had passed. To young Eiko, for whom time had come to a standstill, her mother must have aged in an instant, like in the famous *Urashima Tarō* folk tale.

Tokiko turned to Eiko nervously. '*Ich freue mich, dass Du gekommen bist.* (Thank you for seeing me today),' she said.

Eiko's eyes widened.

'*Wir haben uns lange nicht gesehen. Kannst Du Dir vorstellen? Es ist schon über zwanzig Jahre her, seitdem Du gestorben bist.* (It's been a long time. Can you believe it? It's been over twenty years since you passed away).'

Eiko stood stunned, her lips half-open.

Tokiko smiled. '*Bist Du überrascht?* (Are you surprised?)' Inside, her heart was racing. Was she making any sense? '*Ich kann jetzt ganz einfache Sachen des Alltags auf Deutsch sagen. Ich habe angefangen, Deutsch zu lernen, nachdem ich über fünfzig Jahre alt geworden bin. Karl, Hiroko und alle andere Leute haben mich unterstützt.* (I speak a little German now, just enough for everyday conversation. I started learning after I turned fifty. Karl and Hiroko and the rest of the family have been very supportive).'

'*Ich bin überrascht.* (I'm surprised),' her daughter finally replied. Tokiko was thrilled to hear her response in German.

Eiko sat on the bed and gestured for her mother to join her. '*Ich bin sogar sehr überrascht.* (I am *very* surprised),' she repeated. '*Warum den das?* (Whatever for?)'

'*Nach Deinem Tod war sehr viel los.* (A lot has happened since you passed away),' Tokiko said, reaching for her daughter's hand, which was luminous, smooth and, above all, warm. Her heart filled with gratitude for the go-between, without whom she would never have been able to try out her German. She fought the urge to switch to Japanese.

'After you passed away, Karl invited us to Germany. He wanted your father and me to see where you lived. We were able to meet many of your friends.'

'You did?' Eiko exclaimed.

'They thanked us over and over, saying that if it hadn't been for us, you would never have come to Germany. That we were the reason you all became friends.' Tokiko paused to take a breath as she constructed the sentences in her mind. She knew that her German was choppy and unrefined, but she continued slowly, searching for words.

'Your friends were so kind, yet I felt a bit sad. Here they were thanking us, and we needed Karl to translate. I couldn't even tell them how grateful I was.'

'That's why you learned German?'

Tokiko nodded. 'When I returned to Japan and said that I wanted to learn German, Karl offered to teach me. But he lives in Germany, and I couldn't depend on him forever. So I had Hiroko find me a teacher in Japan.'

Hiroko had sought out a community of German expats in Japan and contacted them. When they, a mother and daughter who spoke no German, showed up to one of their gatherings, the community welcomed them with open arms. Hearing that Tokiko's other daughter once lived in Germany and had married a German man, they celebrated the union, even though Eiko was gone. Tokiko found a German teacher that night.

'Can someone learn to speak German after age fifty?' she asked in Japanese, to which her teacher had replied, also in Japanese, 'Might be hard for most people. But you? Yes. Because I'll be teaching you.' He had nodded assuredly.

Explaining her journey to Eiko, Tokiko shared another surprise. 'I even studied abroad.'

'No! You?'

'Yes,' Tokiko nodded. Though only for six months, the short time abroad was one of the greatest adventures of her life. She had stayed with a host family in Germany who spoke no Japanese; if she was serious about learning the language, that was the way to go, her teacher had said.

The family had welcomed her, saying they had never taken in a student who was almost sixty. They initiated the conversation when she was too shy to speak. 'If you want to learn to speak German, you have to actually speak!' The first month was dizzying.

'At the local language school, I made friends from Taiwan, France, Canada, America. They were all much younger than me, but I enjoyed spending time with them.'

'I can't believe you went by yourself.'

'Because of you. I could never have made the decision on my own.'

Eiko was quiet for a while, taking in her mother's German. She then turned slowly to Tokiko and said, 'Mom, do you remember the cassettes you sent me? Because international calls were so expensive back then, you used to record messages from you, Dad and Hiroko.'

'Yes, it was Hiroko's idea. Dad always said a few words only. He was so nervous!'

It felt like only yesterday that the family had gathered around the tape recorder, embarrassed to speak into the machine while the others listened.

'I loved those tapes,' Eiko said. 'I'm sorry I didn't tell you sooner. Thank you for sending them.'

'Nobody sent *me* tapes when I was in Germany! My stay was short as it was, and the family worried that if they sent me tapes, I would become homesick and come rushing home. After I'd spent so much money to go! Even Karl said I shouldn't be babied, so after he picked me up at the airport, I didn't see him until it was time for me to go home.'

'You and Karl became friends,' Eiko smiled.

When Eiko passed away, Karl had seemed uncomfortable around his new family. And they too hadn't known how to treat him as a member of the family.

'Yes,' Tokiko nodded. 'We're now very good friends. He still sends us flowers on your birthday.'

'Wow.'

'Do you want to know how he's doing?' Tokiko asked, and Eiko gave it some thought. After a while, she replied, '*Nein.*'

Her voice was soft but clear. 'I don't need to hear it. I know he's doing great. Just like you're doing great.'

It was just like her. Eiko was a strong girl.

LYING IN MISATO'S arms, Mei suddenly looked up.

'Mommy.'

'Mmm?' Misato replied, bringing her ear close to her daughter's mouth.

'Is there a baby in there?'

Misato drew back and looked at Mei, who was gently tapping Misato's stomach, like she used to whenever she talked about wanting a little sister. A preschool friend had become a big sister, and she wanted to be one too.

Is my little sister here? Do you have a baby? she asked, sometimes first thing in the morning. *No*, Misato would answer, making her pout. It might be nice to grant her daughter's wish someday. Misato bit her lip to keep from crying in front of her daughter. There had been no baby at the time. But that was no longer the case.

'Yes, there is.'

'Really?' Mei exclaimed, looking from her mother's face to her stomach. 'There is? My little sister is inside?'

'We don't know yet if it's a little sister or brother.'

'Hmm, I want a little sister for sure. Make sure it's a little sister!'

Mei might have asked the question just because she always did. But didn't they say that children had an intuitive sense about these things? She'd heard stories of children cuddling up to pregnant women who weren't yet showing.

When they learned that they were unexpectedly pregnant, Misato and Shoichi had felt both joy and concern. Were they allowed to have another baby? Parents who had killed their little girl?

Let's have Mei meet the baby.

Shoichi was the one who suggested it. And though he too would have loved to see his daughter again, he had stepped aside so Misato could share the news.

'Do you want to touch the baby?'

'Yes!' Mei yelled. She poked Misato's belly with one dainty finger.

Misato giggled, fighting back tears. 'You can touch a little more.'

'I did! She said it feels good.'

'Mei,' Misato said to her daughter. 'Is it OK for Mommy to have this baby?'

She knew it was a cruel question. The child was too young to know what was happening. But she needed to know. She wrapped her arms around her daughter.

'Yes!' Mei cried.

Misato closed her eyes. And kept them closed. She could feel tears welling up behind her eyelids. Maybe this was an illusion. Maybe Mei wasn't real, and the girl in her arms was something she'd dreamed up to make herself feel better.

Still, the tears flowed.

'Thank you,' Misato said. She held Mei tighter. 'Thank you, Mei.'

'Mommy, that hurts!' Mei protested. But she was laughing. *Mommy, Mommy,* she cried happily, throwing her head back and laughing.

Misato tried not to look at the clock as they rolled around on the bed and played for as long as they could.

'Yuna!' Mei had called to Misato's belly. Who was Yuna? 'It's Torata's little sister's name!' Mei said. Torata was Mei's favourite anime character.

'Yuna!' she called over and over.

The sky was starting to grow bright, and Misato thought instinctively, *Oh, I've let her stay up too late.*

'Mommy, I'm sleepy,' Mei said in her arms.

'It's OK, you can sleep,' Misato said softly.

As the morning sun started to shine through the window, Misato felt her arms grow lighter, until there was nothing there.

In her empty arms, Misato could still feel her daughter's body temperature. The parts of her body that her daughter had touched radiated heat and light, both of which would remain with her.

AS LIGHT STARTED to dye the sky white, Eiko switched to Japanese.

'I never thought the day would come when you and I would be speaking to each other in German.'

Tokiko exhaled. Now that they were speaking in Japanese, she no longer had to work her brain. She loosened her shoulders and replied, 'I never would have learned if it weren't for you.' Which also meant, *If you hadn't died.* If her daughter had been alive and well, this day would never have come.

Speaking to Eiko in German had been a years-long dream, but she would give it all up for the chance to have her daughter back again.

'I'm glad we were able to talk today,' Tokiko said, 'but my real wish is something else.'

'Your real wish?'

'Do you remember when you made a presentation at an academic conference in Germany? You sounded so confident up there.' Eiko blinked. Tokiko continued, 'You recorded your speech. Karl told us that you were thinking of sending it to us.'

'Oh,' Eiko nodded. 'That's right. I thought of sending it but didn't. I wanted you all to know I was doing great, but it was just audio, and the whole presentation was in German.'

'Karl told us. He looked for it so he could share it with us.'

Tokiko had listened to the tape with her family, and though they couldn't understand it, hearing Eiko's clear voice filled them with joy. Now that Tokiko had studied the language, she could understand most of its content, even some of the more technical words.

'If I could be granted one wish, it would have been to see you up there giving your speech. I would have loved a glimpse.'

The light was starting to illuminate the sky. It was almost morning. Tokiko fixed her eyes on her daughter, wanting to hold on to every feature.

Tokiko was seventy-four, and she might be joining Eiko before long. Which was why she wanted to share her new skills now, as a memory of this life.

'Thank you for everything, Eiko.'

Eiko's silhouette was starting to fade. 'I'm the one who should be saying thanks.' She smiled. 'Thank you for coming to see me,' she said in German.

Her body was growing transparent.

'*Auf Wiedersehen,*' Eiko said one final time.

Tokiko blinked, and Eiko was gone. The room fell silent. Left alone, Tokiko said in Japanese, 'Yes, let's meet again.'

SHORTLY PAST FIVE in the morning, a woman in a slim pantsuit, looking stunning, appeared in the lobby. Ayumi knew who it was the moment he saw her – it was Hiroko, Tokiko's other daughter and Eiko's younger sister. She too saw Ayumi and gave him a slight nod, then took a seat on the sofa.

Ayumi wondered if he should go over and say hello, but decided to stay where he was and wait for Tokiko to come downstairs.

Misato's husband Shoichi was also waiting. He had sat the whole night with his hands pressed in front of his face, never once looking over at Ayumi, only willing the time to pass.

At a little past six o'clock, Misato Shigeta stepped out of the elevator. Shoichi saw her before Ayumi did, and he shot to his feet.

Misato's face was drenched in tears.

'Misato,' Shoichi called and took her in his arms.

'I saw her,' she said.

Dangling from her bag was the officially issued keychain that pregnant mothers often hung from their bags to let people know they were expecting. She'd hidden the keychain on her way up to the hotel room.

'That's good,' Shoichi rasped. They stood in an embrace until, finally, Misato dabbed her eyes and looked at Ayumi. 'Thank . . . you.' She bowed her head. 'Thank you . . . very much.'

'Oh no . . .' Ayumi replied, leading them to a nearby sofa. Just then, he heard a voice call out, 'Mom.' He turned to see Tokiko walking out of the elevator. Hiroko ran to her side.

Ayumi had never had two clients come into contact before, and he didn't know who to attend to first. As he started towards Tokiko, the old woman exclaimed happily, 'Oh, Hiroko! You're here. Thanks for coming.' She didn't seem to have seen Ayumi.

'Seriously, Mom. Did you stay up all night? Aren't you tired?'

'I'm fine! You know I'm a night owl!'

Hiroko led her mother to a sofa, walking right past Ayumi in the middle of the lobby.

'Oh?' Tokiko's eyes landed on the couple at the next bench over. Misato had regained her composure and was now sitting up without her husband's help.

Tokiko regarded the Shigetas gently and said, 'Are you expecting?' Tokiko's eyes had landed on Misato's maternity keychain. 'Congratulations. I hope you have a happy, healthy baby.'

Misato bit her lip. 'I'm actually very scared.' She looked up at the elderly woman, whom she had just met, and said, 'I don't know if I deserve to be a mother.'

For a split second, Tokiko's expression froze. Hiroko also took a sharp breath in. But the next moment, the old woman said in a bright, sunny voice, 'Oh my goodness, I know you will do great. Everything will be absolutely fine.' She gave Misato a light tap on the shoulders. 'Now if you're anything like me, I'd be worried. But the two of you? You'll be just fine! How exciting.'

'Uh, Mom,' Hiroko said. 'I don't think they need to hear this. Let's go.' She prodded her mother gently.

'Oh, I'm so sorry,' Tokiko said, and smiled goodbye to the younger couple. She still hadn't seen Ayumi. 'I would love some water,' she said to her daughter as they slowly made their way towards the lounge.

Ayumi didn't know whether the exchange between the two mothers had been fate in action. But he wanted to believe there was a reason the two parties had met.

He watched as the mother and daughter leaned into each other. 'Do you want to have breakfast here?' They appeared to have forgotten all about Ayumi. But perhaps Hiroko had subtly led her mother away. He would catch up with Tokiko in a moment.

He walked over to the Shigetas, who were watching Tokiko and her daughter.

'What a beautiful pair. I wonder why she said she would be worried?' Misato murmured.

'Yeah,' Shoichi said.

They had no way of knowing that Tokiko had also lost a daughter. And to those who didn't know the Shigetas' story, they looked like a happy young couple who was eagerly awaiting their baby's birth.

As the morning light streamed into the lobby, Ayumi cast his gaze upwards, sending a message to Mei and Eiko, the two big sisters.

He hoped they were watching, wherever they were.

4

The Rule of the Only Daughter

*E*VERY DAY *I think about what he would do in my situation. I almost wish he would come and yell at me for doing it wrong.*

'NO KID WILL go for this, right?'

The question seemed to be directed at him, and Ayumi looked up from the form he was filling out to see the owner of Torino Workshop with something in his hand. It was a wooden dog-shaped toy.

'This,' Taisho showed it to him. He wound it up and the feet made a buzzing sound as it was placed on the desk.

'Is it a new product?'

It didn't look like something Ayumi's company had

147

commissioned. Their projects with Torino Workshop usually proceeded like this: Ayumi approached them with a design or sketch, and after discussing the details with Taisho, he left the creation process pretty much up to him. Once the toy was completed, Ayumi's company took over and distributed it to toy stores. Every once in a while Taisho asked them to take on a toy he had designed, but those occasions were rare. When he did come to them with an item, they knew it would be exquisite, and many did in fact become long-sellers.

Any toy made from wood can technically be called a 'wooden toy', but the quality of a product depends on who made it and what *feel* they have infused into it. Children are drawn instinctively to certain toys, ignoring the ones that fail to hold their interest. In the wooden toy industry, demand was low for shiny new objects. Long-sellers were the true winners.

The soft contours of the toy in Taisho's hand gave it a certain charm, and there was a string attached for children to pull as they walked. But something didn't feel right. It didn't quite have the Torino Workshop touch.

'You might call it that. What's your honest opinion?'

'Hmm . . .' Ayumi set his pen down and took the toy from Taisho. 'This stop-go, stop-go motion . . . I would make its movements a little slower. Slow enough for two- and three-year-old kids to be able to follow with their eyes.'

'I agree.'

'And . . . the tail.'

A small wooden ball was attached to the end of the tail, and though the braided cord was secured to the body, it still made Ayumi nervous.

'If we were handling this toy, we would need to change the tail. To prevent the risk of swallowing if the ball comes off.'

Ayumi had learned in his two years at the company that with children's toys, design took a back seat to safety. It wasn't like Taisho to allow this.

'Yeah . . . that's the other thing,' Taisho mumbled, scratching his head.

It was unusual for him to sound so indecisive. Taisho was an artisan who took pride in his creations, and even when he and Ayumi disagreed on how to *sell* a toy, he never spoke negatively about the toy itself.

'But . . .' Ayumi said, suddenly sympathetic towards the dog. 'It has a kind face, which I think kids will be drawn to.'

'No, no, it's OK. It needs to be redone. This just won't cut it.'

'Are you sure?'

'Sorry to take you away from your work,' Taisho said, shaking his head and smiling.

'Oh, that's no problem . . .'

Ayumi glanced at Taisho's work desk in the corner of

the studio, which was filled with colourful block puzzles, a pushcart shaped like a whale, and other toys Ayumi had never seen before. Were they all new products? They looked like they could be put on the market immediately.

'Did you make all of those?'

'Hm?'

'Sorry, those. Behind you.'

'Oh ...'

Following Ayumi's gaze, Taisho picked up a block. The small colourful blocks were designed to be placed in wooden frames shaped like a yacht or a house. Ayumi's company had handled a similar puzzle before, made by a company in Switzerland, if he remembered right.

'If the block puzzle doesn't have a distributor yet, is that something we might be able to take on? The rolling ball structure next to it is beautiful too.'

The rolling ball structure, or *Kugelbahn* in German, was an item in which marbles rolled along a wooden rail. Taisho picked up a block puzzle and murmured, 'I guess this is pretty decent. I may take you up on that someday. I can't make any promises, but if the time comes, I'll let you know.'

'That would be great. Thank you.'

'Anyway, enough about that. Today is about *your* first toy. I'm looking forward to seeing it on store shelves.'

Ayumi tapped the turtle toy on the desk. Its green shell

lifted slightly off the body so that it could be spun around. He had been working with Torino Workshop on this for months now and the colour was of particular concern. He had asked Taisho, as well as his own boss, even Anna for their opinions, before finally committing to green.

He had made a trip to the studio today to thank Taisho in person and to discuss next steps.

'You must be excited.'

'It's more disbelief than anything. I can't believe it's happening.'

Torino Workshop had produced so many toys in the years it had been in business that Ayumi's first design probably meant little. Still, he couldn't wait to send them a photo of the toy on store shelves.

'You said before that you might want to make toys someday, not just design them,' Taisho said. 'Do you still feel that way?'

'Yes,' Ayumi replied. 'But . . .'

He remembered making the comment to Taisho when he was just starting out. He couldn't believe he had the audacity.

'I'm embarrassed to have said that, to you of all people. I know now that this is a craft that takes years to learn, not something any amateur can do . . .'

'No, I think you have a real knack for it.'

Ayumi widened his eyes. Taisho picked up the toy dog again.

'You knew just by looking what didn't work. Talent is a cruel thing. Sometimes people have it and don't know it, and other times, it's just not there. I've been at this for a long time. Some things you can cover with practice and effort, but nothing can be done about talent. It's a sensibility. And you have a sense for these things.'

Ayumi felt a thrill race through his body. Taisho's words would buoy him for the next several *years*.

'Thank you . . . so much.' His own voice sounded far away.

'If you're interested, I can teach you the basics of wood-working. Your work at the company comes first, of course, but on days like this when we finish up early, do you want to play around a little, get a feel for the wood?'

'Really?'

Taisho seemed surprised by Ayumi's enthusiasm. 'Yeah. If it's something you're interested in. As you can see, we're a tiny studio. We have no other staff members or apprentices. Feel free to use whatever's here.'

'That means so much to me.' Ayumi stood and bowed at the waist.

'No need to go overboard,' Taisho said, laughing. 'Shibuya-san used to tinker with the wood when he visited too. We worked on wooden chairs and shelves and things together.'

By *Shibuya-san*, he meant Ryo Shibuya, Ayumi's father.

Though Ayumi had virtually no memory of his father, the people of this studio had collaborated with him on several occasions. Nao once told him about a paper crane that Ayumi's father had folded for her.

'I wish I could recruit you, but I can't afford to pay you what your company does,' Taisho joked, patting the shell of Ayumi's toy turtle with his rugged hands. 'I like this turtle. I think it'll do well.'

That was when they heard Nao's voice call out, 'Dad!'

'What's up?'

As she walked into the studio, the late afternoon sun shone in through the window and on to her light brown hair, which was pulled into a loose ponytail. 'Pardon the interruption,' she said, smiling at Ayumi. 'Mom says to see if Shibuya-san would like to stay for dinner. She's going to start frying the tempura.'

Taisho looked at Ayumi, who hesitated for a moment. He had been visiting the studio for a few years now, and for the first year or so, he had politely declined their invitations. But once they joked, 'It's ruder to say no!' he gladly started joining them for their homecooked meals.

'I would love to.'

'That's what I'm talking about,' Taisho grinned.

'My dad loves it when you're here. You'll have to take a later shinkansen. Is that OK?' Nao asked.

'There are a lot of great hot springs around here too,' Taisho boomed. 'You should stay overnight!'

'I think that's going a bit far,' Ayumi said.

Nao and Taisho laughed.

THE DAY HAD come. Ayumi's first product would be hitting the shelves of a toy store in the K Garden shopping centre near his office. He had asked to deliver the products to the store himself.

The toy turtles had arrived at the office last night from Torino Workshop, and his hands trembled as he opened the box. He unwrapped each turtle gently, charmed by their expressions.

He was eager to show Anna and her parents. As well as his uncle, aunt and cousin Akane, with whom he'd lived until college. But the person with whom he wished to share this moment most was his grandmother Aiko. He remembered wanting to show her everything he made or did as a child, not because it made her happy, but because it lit up *his* world.

'Is it OK if I take a photo?' he asked the shop clerk. 'I want to send it to the people at the workshop.'

'Of course. Be my guest.'

'Thank you. Can I also post the photo on our company website?'

The shop clerk smiled and nodded as Ayumi took several photos with his phone camera. Just then, the device rang in his hand. The screen showed that it was his boss, the company president.

A bad feeling crept up, though he couldn't explain why. Perhaps because his boss was calling from his cell phone and not the office. There was nothing urgent, as far as Ayumi knew. 'Excuse me for a moment,' he said to the clerk before taking the call.

'Ayumi? Can you talk?' his boss said.

'Sure!' he replied, trying to sound as casual as possible. 'Is anything the matter?'

His boss took a sharp breath.

'Torino-san passed away.'

'WHAT!?'

The shop clerk jumped and looked at Ayumi, alarmed. 'When you say Torino-san, do you mean Taisho? Why? You're kidding, right?'

'I don't believe it either, but it's true.'

Ayumi looked up at the toy he had just photographed.

He had seen Taisho just two weeks ago. Had even stayed for dinner. He had looked happy and healthy then.

'It was a heart attack,' Ayumi's boss said. 'He had a heart condition.'

*

A WHILE LATER, Ayumi stood in line with his boss and colleagues to pay his respects at a hall near Torino Workshop where the memorial service was being held. He'd grown used to wearing suits now that he was a working professional, but it had been a while since he last wore a black necktie.

The last funeral Ayumi had attended was for his grandmother, when he was still in college.

How could he not have noticed?

Taisho had been dealing with a heart condition.

'He first found out about it in his early forties, and he normally took medication for it. I'd heard that he had it under control . . .' Ayumi's boss Imura said. Ayumi was in shock. He'd visited the studio so many times, working closely with Taisho, and he hadn't known anything about it.

No, he hadn't been *told* about it. His boss knew. He could almost hear Taisho saying to Imura, who was about the same age, 'It's really nothing to worry about!' But Taisho had kept it from Ayumi, probably because he was young and inexperienced.

But couldn't Ayumi have paid better attention? They'd shared so many meals together, in the Torino home, at a neighbourhood restaurant, and after each meal, Taisho had always taken his medicine. Ayumi had watched him do it but had dismissed it, thinking it was normal for someone who was almost sixty to be taking a few pills.

He listened to me go on and on about my problems. Their working relationship had been entirely one-sided. Ayumi couldn't be counted on.

Amid the nonstop chanting of the Buddhist priest and the smell of incense that permeated the air, Ayumi felt paralysed as he stood in the line of visitors paying their respects.

Inching closer to the front of the line, his eyes landed on Nao and her mother standing next to a large photograph of Taisho. In the photo, Taisho wore his usual work apron and the wide, generous smile he was known for – they'd had no time to take a formal photograph. The sunny photo looked out of place surrounded by rows of flowers in the funeral home.

The day after they received news of Taisho's passing, Ayumi and his boss had jumped on the shinkansen to Karuizawa.

Torino Workshop was still and quiet in the late afternoon hours. The fresh smell of lumber and wood greeted them as they stepped into the studio. Nao spotted them right away. 'Shibuya-san. And Imura-san too.' Her face was ashen, her cheeks so pale they were nearly transparent. She looked all cried out.

Ayumi knew what one was supposed to say at a time like this.

I'm sorry for your loss. My deepest condolences.

But the words got stuck in his throat.

'Nao-san . . .'

As he lowered he head in a deep bow, Nao's mother appeared, looking several sizes smaller herself. After she greeted them, she said, 'Please see him . . . if you would like.'

They had brought Taisho home from the hospital, and he lay before them now, looking as though he were sleeping. 'Taisho,' Ayumi called out shakily. The man looked as if he could rise at any moment and joke, 'Why so blue?' Or come up behind them and quip, 'Hey, don't stare so hard. Poor guy's sleeping.'

Ayumi couldn't believe he was gone.

'He had a condition we knew he would be dealing with for the rest of his life, but he always said it wasn't something that would worsen overnight,' Okusan said. She placed her hand on Taisho's chest, and her eyes welled up again. 'Who would have thought . . .'

She started to sob.

'Mom,' Nao said, patting her gently on the back. She didn't shed a tear, at least not there in that moment.

*

'Thank you for coming, Shibuya-san.'

Nao called to Ayumi as he was about to head home. Ayumi shook his head, wishing he could be of some help to her and her family.

'Your first design . . .' Nao said.

Ayumi stopped.

'Did you get to see it on store shelves?'

Her mouth softened into a smile. Ayumi nodded, tears springing to his eyes.

'I'm glad,' Nao said. 'Can you send me a photo if you can? I want to show Dad.'

Taisho had collapsed in late afternoon the day Ayumi's product arrived at his office. Watching Nao wrap the items the day before, he'd chuckled, 'He's going to cry when he gets this.'

The funeral line moved forward.

Ayumi heard someone say, not for the first time that day, 'She's their only daughter.' He thought about what that meant. Nao had no siblings, nobody with whom to discuss what to do next.

Ayumi didn't know any of the funeral attendees, but he could see Taisho had developed bonds with countless people over the years, just as he had with Ayumi.

'Why him?'

'He was so good at what he did.'

'Always there to help anyone who needed it.'

And then he heard, '. . . He said young people these days even ask what colour a product should be. Times really have changed. Back in our day, we had to decide everything for ourselves.'

Ayumi turned towards the voice but couldn't tell who was speaking. Someone around Taisho's age, perhaps one of his colleagues.

Were they talking about him? He'd asked Taisho for advice on the colour of the turtle shell. Repeatedly. Taisho had considered the options with him and finally laughed, 'You don't give up, do you?'

Ayumi felt his chest grow cold and his body temperature drop. Had Taisho been annoyed with him? Maybe he had complained about him to his inner circle, the people he trusted most.

I wish I could apologize. For getting a big head, for thinking he knew what he was talking about.

He looked again at Nao and her mother in their black funeral clothes, bowing to visitors like automated dolls. They looked almost unrecognizable.

As Ayumi and Imura approached the front of the line, his boss said gently, 'We're deeply sorry for your loss.' Ayumi bowed silently. He had assumed that Nao and her mother would bow back in the same mechanical way they had been greeting everyone else. But when Nao's eyes met his, her face crumpled.

'Shibuya-san,' she said.

'Ayumi,' her mother whispered next to her.

Ayumi thought about Torino Workshop, the studio in the woods, and a sharp pain pierced his chest. The studio with the woody smell, big windows and sunbeams streaming in from every angle. His father's chair. Taisho was supposed to start teaching him the basics of woodworking.

He looked at Nao and Okusan, nodded, and bowed his head. Until that day, he'd only ever seen Nao in an apron, running around the studio taking care of administrative duties. But today her hair was down, and she wore a strand of pearls around her neck. She still looked lovely, but her despair and exhaustion were painful to witness.

'I'm sorry,' he croaked. Nao gave a small nod, her eyes stained with tears. It was all they had time for. Ayumi stepped towards Taisho's photograph, and with shaking fingers, he picked up an incense stick.

Taisho, he said silently. *There was so much I was hoping you would teach me.*

*

TWO WEEKS AFTER the funeral, Ayumi received a call from Nao.

Once things settled down, he had been hoping to visit the studio and sit down with Nao and her mother to talk about Taisho, and to discuss the studio. Of course, things would never settle down. He knew the death of a loved one never fully became a thing of the past.

Nao was already seated when Ayumi arrived at the cafe in Tokyo's Ebisu neighbourhood.

After the funeral, he had been thinking about when he could go to Karuizawa without inconveniencing the Torinos. Thankfully, Nao contacted him first and said, 'I'm sorry to call you out of the blue. I know you must be busy.'

'I know *you* must be busy,' Ayumi had said.

'I'm actually going to be in Tokyo shortly,' Nao said.

Torino Workshop did business with many clients in Tokyo aside from Ayumi's company, and he imagined that Nao was paying each a visit to discuss how to move forward.

'Things have finally calmed down a little,' she continued. 'Funeral preparations were hectic, and I barely remember a thing about it, but now that that's over, there's not a whole lot left for us to do.' She almost sounded as though she wished things had remained hectic.

Sitting in the cafe now, the colour seemed to have returned

to her cheeks, although she had lost weight, and her smile still betrayed her sorrow. But perhaps she was slowly coming to terms with her father's death, which was true of Ayumi as well.

Their coffee arrived. They each took a sip and Ayumi finally said, 'The studio . . .'

'My mother and I have decided to continue with my father's projects, at least the ones we can handle. Thankfully, he wasn't working on anything urgent.' Nao placed her cup on the table and looked at Ayumi. 'I'm glad we finished yours in time.'

'Right . . .'

He was proud and grateful to have completed the project, to both his and Taisho's satisfaction. No compromises. But there was so much more he had yet to learn.

As a client himself, Ayumi knew that people came to Torino Workshop because they wanted to work with Taisho. Following his death, he imagined that the workshop had parted ways with a number of clients. Ayumi's own company would likely need to find another woodworking studio for future orders.

Nao seemed to read his mind.

'Of course, there were some projects and offers we had to turn down, knowing my mother and I couldn't handle them. It's sad, but there's nothing we can do.'

'What about the studio?'

Taisho had been the sole creative force behind it. Nao had managed administration and her mother of course played a key role, but nobody could take over the creative part of the business.

Nao's cheeks tightened, her eyes turning serious. 'Shibuya-san.'

Ayumi sat up straight.

'I'm here today to discuss that. I appreciate your offer to come all the way out to Karuizawa, but I wanted to talk about this without my mother. About the studio . . . um . . . did my father ever say anything to you about it? Or . . . anything about me?'

'About you?'

Nao's eyes were fixed on him. 'Did he ever say anything about me taking over the studio someday?'

'I'D BEEN ASKING him for years if I could one day take over,' Nao said. 'I've been wanting him to teach me woodworking, which I've watched him do since I was a girl.'

Ayumi suddenly remembered the scene he'd witnessed last year as he was leaving the studio. Taisho and Nao were discussing something, and he thought he'd heard Taisho say,

You need to let it go. Was that—? Had Nao asked her father to teach her the craft?

'I'd always loved the toys my father made. Not just the toys. The clocks and planters and everything else. I used to tell my friends that my dad could make anything out of wood.'

Ayumi recalled seeing a wooden clock in the shape of a violin at the studio. Nao had grown up surrounded by her father's creations. When she was a little girl, she explained, he once made a wooden tower and said to her, 'Here, drop this ball in.' She placed a marble into a slot and was rewarded with the crisp, light sound of wood – like a xylophone – as the ball fell through the tower.

'I thought he was a magician,' Nao said.

When she became captivated by a children's TV programme that featured various toys, devices and contraptions, he'd said, 'That's easy to make,' and created an original rolling ball structure just for Nao.

'My school projects were always woodwork. Some came out so good that my teachers and friends thought my father helped me, but he never touched any of my projects, only coached me verbally.'

It didn't take long for her to decide that this would be her career path, and one day, when the time came, she would take over his studio.

'I was in my final year of high school the first time I brought it up with him,' she said, looking at Ayumi. 'I said that I wanted to learn from him, and hopefully take over the business someday. I told him that I wouldn't be going to college.'

But Taisho had objected. Regardless of what she ended up doing with her life, he said, she had to go out and experience the world while she had the chance.

'He told me to stop using the studio as an excuse to get out of studying for college entrance exams. When he put it that way, I did wonder if that's what I was doing. I wanted to learn the craft, yes, but I also *really* didn't want to go through entrance exam hell,' Nao laughed.

'That sounds like something he would say.'

'Doesn't it? He said if I thought he was going to go easy on me because I was family, I had another thing coming. So I found a school where I could study design, and I left home to go to college.'

After graduating, she approached her father again. Ayumi thought the situation sounded ideal. What more could Taisho ask for? But again he refused.

'He said he wouldn't teach me because I would one day get married and leave. He was really old-fashioned in that way.' She bit her lip. 'But I wasn't going to take no for an answer either, so finally he told me to do administration for the workshop so I could learn what the business entailed.'

'Wow.'

Ayumi hadn't known any of this and thought Nao simply preferred the office work.

'Shibuya-san,' Nao said. 'Shortly before he died, I approached him one last time.' He saw a flash of desperation in her eyes. 'I thought I had a better understanding of the studio. I learned what kind of work he did and why people came to him. And I learned how hard, and valuable, my father's work was. Which is why I didn't want Torino Workshop to end with him.'

'You asked him once more?'

'Yes.' Nao bit her lip and looked at Ayumi. Her eyes welled up.

'He said he would think about it. And then a little while later, he asked me to go on a drive with him. He said, let's go look at some trees this weekend.'

'Trees?'

'To Iiyama . . . that's where we order our lumber. He said he wanted to talk to me about something, which I assumed meant we would discuss my apprenticeship.' Her eyes clouded over. 'But then two days before our drive, he collapsed. And that was it . . .'

Ayumi swallowed quietly.

'I never found out what he wanted to say.'

'But that's . . .' Ayumi wasn't a member of the family and

didn't know how much he was allowed to say. He said it anyway. 'Taisho had to have wanted to pass the business on to you. He invited you to go and see the trees, which is the lifeline of the business.'

'I thought, maybe, yes. But there's no way of knowing now. Dad may have had other plans.'

Ayumi noticed the switch from 'my father' to 'Dad'.

'I should have asked,' she said. 'That's all I needed to do. But I figured I could ask him tomorrow, or the day after that. I never imagined that he would just disappear.'

She looked at him pleadingly and said, 'Did he ever discuss this kind of thing with you?' The twinkle had vanished from her eyes.

'I'm sorry . . . no. We rarely discussed anything that wasn't work-related.'

No matter how close he felt to the family, he'd come to realize over the past month and a half that he was a stranger. Someone who couldn't be trusted with essential information.

'I see.' Nao looked visibly disappointed. Worried that she might get up and leave, he asked, 'What does your mother say about the situation?'

'She hasn't heard anything either.'

Ayumi thought about why Nao wouldn't want to discuss this in front of her mother. Perhaps Okusan wasn't thrilled about her only daughter taking over the studio either. Getting through Taisho's current projects was one thing; trying to cultivate new work when her husband was no longer around was another thing entirely.

'Running a business is hard work,' Nao said, looking down again. 'My mother probably had something to do with the decision not to let me apprentice right away. But she says she hasn't heard anything from my father. She wasn't even aware that I'd asked him again to teach me.'

'I see . . .'

'Which is why I thought maybe you might know something. I'm sorry to take up your time.'

'Why did you think I might know something?'

'Because you and my father got along so well. He really liked you. I thought maybe he'd confided in you, guy to guy. I'm so sorry.'

'No, I'm sorry for not being able to help.'

He said young people these days even ask what colour a product should be. Times really have changed. Back in our day, we had to decide everything for ourselves.

The words he'd heard at the funeral came back to him, making his chest tighten.

'I think we're going to have to close up shop,' Nao said.

Ayumi imagined how much she must have deliberated before she could bring herself to say those words out loud.

'We'll never know what he was thinking, whether he

wanted to keep it going or shut it down after he retired. Whatever the case, he's no longer here. Once we get through the projects he left behind, I think we have no choice but to close.'

'Right . . .'

Ayumi wanted to tell her to keep the studio open, but he couldn't go around saying whatever came to him. They were talking about running a business.

'Thank you for everything. All the work you've done with us over the years,' Nao said.

'No, thank you. Truly.'

He had no more ongoing projects with Torino Workshop, which meant he might never see Nao again. She was likely aware of that too.

'I hope to visit you again, to pay my respects to Taisho.'

'Please do,' Nao nodded.

They stood up from their seats, paid for their drinks and stepped outside.

'OK, I'll be seeing you,' Nao said.

As she was about to walk away, Ayumi instinctively reached for the hem of her coat. 'Um . . .'

He finally knew what he'd been wanting to say. Listening to her story, he'd even started to say it a few times.

Would you like to see him again?

'Yes?' Nao turned around, surprised. 'What's the matter?'

He took a deep breath. 'Oh, uh . . .' he stammered. 'It's nothing. Please take care.'

Nao's eyes softened. 'You too,' she said, and turned towards the station.

What was I thinking? Ayumi thought. *She's not a client.* She didn't ask to see the go-between.

AYUMI, WHETHER A *person can connect with the go-between is a matter of fate. It's either meant to be, or it isn't.*

He could still hear his grandmother's voice when he closed his eyes, and imagine her wrinkly hands, her eyes that saw right through him, and her smile. The warmth of that smile.

He wished he could ask her now. If it was true that some people could never connect with the go-between while the opportunity practically fell into the laps of others, what did that say about his relationship with the Torino family? The fact that he knew Nao, and that he happened to be able to set up a meeting between the living and the dead . . . did those things fall under the category of fate?

Ayumi watched the city zip by from the train window on his way to the Akiyama house. The weekday night train was packed, and the city lights outside of the window overlapped with the mirrored reflections of passengers.

As the go-between, his job was to stand in the shoes of someone who'd lost a loved one.

Though he had become accustomed to encountering death on a regular basis, this was the first since his grandmother that felt personal to him.

Ayumi had decided years ago that when the time came for him to ask the go-between for a meeting, he would ask to see his grandmother, but not because he needed anything from her. They had shared numerous meaningful conversations before she died, and he'd been able to take his time to say goodbye. She had given him the time he needed to process her passing, which said more about her than it did him.

He remembered the day he officially stepped into the role.

Once he became the go-between, Ayumi would no longer be able to meet anyone by request himself, and his grandmother, who was the go-between at the time, had offered to set up a meeting with anybody he wished before handing him the reins. After deliberating for weeks, he'd told her, 'It won't be for a long time, but once I pass the go-between to someone else, I'm going to request a meeting with you. I'll probably be all old and grey by then too.'

'I'm not old and grey,' his grandmother had shot back.

'I'm going to request you,' Ayumi said again. 'I'm reserving you now, so don't see anyone before me, OK?'

'Save it for somebody else. Your life is just getting started, and you have no idea what's in store for you. You'll get married, have kids. You'll forget about me in no time.'

'Maybe. But for now, let's just say I'll choose you.' He didn't know if his grandmother's testiness was an attempt to mask her joy. He laughed. 'If I still want to see you when I'm old, it's proof that I lived a nice, peaceful life, right? So wait for me.'

'... Ah, true. OK,' his grandmother nodded.

A while later, his grandmother had said to him, 'If you get married in the future—'

'That's not happening anytime soon.'

'I said *if*. If you get married, I hope you'll be able to tell the person everything.'

Still a teenager then, Ayumi had been horrified by the thought of marriage.

'Everything?'

'*Everything*. That you're the go-between. About your father and mother. Everything.'

He didn't know why she'd brought this up. What she was talking about was years in the future. Had his grandmother known that she wouldn't be able to stay by his side for much longer?

*

Two years after that conversation, his grandmother, who had been in and out of the hospital for some time, could no longer leave her bed.

When Ayumi was in his second year of college, his uncle received a late-night call from the hospital.

The previous year, his grandmother's brother – Ayumi's great-uncle Sadayuki – had died of lung cancer. 'My big brother's gone ahead and is prepping for my arrival,' his grandmother had joked then.

Holding her hand at Sadayuki's funeral, Ayumi had asked, 'Do you wish you could talk to him again?'

'No,' she said without hesitation. 'I said my goodbye. I have no regrets. And he would say the same thing, if it were me in that coffin and he was standing here with you.'

'Don't joke. Geez . . .'

'It could have been me having the funeral today. Just as easily. That's life.'

Ayumi's grandmother never regained consciousness after the phone call. Her condition had taken a turn for the worse and she was starting to fade away. The family rushed to hospital to find that she could no longer speak behind her oxygen mask.

Ayumi didn't know at the time which conversation with her was his last, but he had no regrets. Each time he left her

side, he told himself it could be the last time. His grandmother had helped to create that space for him.

In the car on the way home from the hospital that night, his
aunt, who was behind the wheel, told Ayumi and his cousin
Akane what his grandmother's illness was for the first time.
She and her husband had kept it from them so as not to
frighten them. Ayumi sensed that his aunt wanted them
to have a chance to say goodbye.

'I think tomorrow could be our last day with her,' his
aunt said. 'I love your grandmother so much. We've lived
together for a very long time now, but can you believe we've
never had a fight?'

His aunt and grandmother were great people, but they
were also human, and it was only natural to clash once or
twice over the span of twenty years. What amazed Ayumi
was the strength in his aunt's words. *We never fought.* That
was how she chose to remember their relationship.

His grandmother died the next morning. While Ayumi
did cry at her memorial service, he was able to keep his emotions largely under control.

*It could have been me having the funeral today. Just as easily.
That's life.*

He sometimes felt she could still be alive somewhere in the
world, going about her business as usual. Which was why he

didn't feel the need to see her – at least not yet. If his life continued without major drama, and one day, years down the line, he found himself wanting to see her, that's when he might request a meeting, so he could give her an update on his life.

His farewell with his grandmother wasn't the kind of ending where he was left with unanswered questions, undiscussed matters, like Nao was experiencing now. He thought about the magnitude of Nao's loss, and his heart ached.

The train jolted to a stop as the station name was announced over the loudspeakers. Ayumi let out a breath, then weaved through the crowded train to the door.

'HMMMM, I DON'T know. That sounds like overstepping to me.'

Ayumi had finished dinner with the Akiyamas and was now helping Anna with her homework. As he checked the answers to her math problems, he gave a quick rundown of the situation with Nao. He told Anna that someone he'd worked closely with had passed away. That the man and his family had treated Ayumi like one of them. That their daughter was left with questions that only her father could answer. And that he wondered whether he should tell her about the go-between.

Nao may never have heard of the go-between, not even

as a rumour. It was an absurd story, but would she believe it coming from him? Or would it seem unrealistic *because* it had come from him?

Ayumi had asked Anna for help once before when a girl he knew was directly associated with a request that had come in, and he had hesitated about becoming involved. Anna had met with the client in his place.

But this time, Anna shook her head before Ayumi could finish.

'You think it's overstepping?' Ayumi asked.

'Yes. The girl you're talking about isn't a client. She didn't seek out the go-between. She's just someone you, Ayumi, happen to know in real life.'

'True, but if we're acquainted in real life, isn't that fate in a way? Whether she knows it or not, she happens to be in close proximity to the go-between.'

Anna said, 'Ohhhhh,' nodding. She then snorted. He often let her precocious reactions slide, seeing as how she was the head of the household, but her laugh rubbed him the wrong way today.

'What?' he asked.

'Ayumi, you're not getting a big head, are you? This girl happens to know Ayumi Shibuya, not the go-between. She knows *you*. That's all.'

As much as it irritated him, she was right. He had met Nao and her family, not as the go-between, but as his regular plain self. To think of himself as having a great power was, as Anna had said, just him with a swollen head. Still, it wasn't easy to separate the two.

Anna looked up from her homework and said, 'Also, can you handle it?'

'Handle what?'

'Revealing to the girl, and to her father, that you're the go-between.'

'That . . .'

Was something he had been thinking about.

'You know you're never going to be able to go back, right?' Anna said sharply. 'Even if I step in for you again, hiding the fact that you're the go-between. If she meets with her father, you're going to learn more about her than you might want to know in real life. Using the go-between means no more hiding behind masks and polite talk. Once you become involved in that part of a person's life, you'll never be able to go back to the way things were. Whether the reunion is a happy one or goes completely awry. Your relationship with this person will be changed forever.'

Ayumi was struck not only by the girl but by his great-uncle for appointing her. He hadn't been able to pinpoint what had been bothering him, but Anna had laid it out for him. And she was right. He'd once arranged a meeting for two high school classmates, and he was never able to view them in the same light again.

Say that Nao had come to him with a request for the go-between. In that case, Ayumi would summon Taisho to relay Nao's message. He too would get to see Taisho again. The thought of reuniting with the man he admired and respected, someone he thought he would never see again. What he wouldn't give for that opportunity.

On the other hand, he thought, *Was that really true?*

He remembered the line he'd heard at the funeral. *Young people these days . . .*

Perhaps there were some doors that were better left closed.

'Yeah . . . I guess . . .'

Seeing Ayumi go quiet, Anna let out a long sigh. 'Fine . . . OK. How about we try it on one condition?'

'A condition?'

'I'm going to be honest. I don't know for sure whether this person is meant to see the go-between. Which is why . . . I'll wait. You don't work with the studio any more, right?'

'Right.'

'You have no ongoing projects with them. If she contacts you one more time, then maybe it *is* meant to be. If she calls and you feel pulled to tell her the truth, I say go ahead.'

Ayumi didn't know how she spoke with such confidence.

'Did the solution come to you as the head of the house?'

'Nope. Instinct,' she said, then went back to the math questions Ayumi had gone over. 'No way! How is this wrong?' she exclaimed.

Smarter than most adults, Ayumi marvelled. *Yet you can't do math.*

WHEN NAO'S NAME popped up on his phone a few weeks after his talk with Anna, Ayumi realized he was nervous.

'Hi, Shibuya-san, it's Nao. Do you have a minute?'

There was determination in her voice, as though she'd made a decision. Ayumi too knew what he needed to tell her. 'I was hoping to call you too,' he replied. 'How have you been?'

Nao offered to come out to Tokyo, but he said he would make the trip to Karuizawa this time. Now that Taisho was gone, he no longer had a reason to visit Torino Workshop, but there was no better place for their discussion. Nao didn't refuse. 'OK. I look forward to seeing you.'

As Ayumi walked up the path to the studio, even the sunlight that shone from between the trees seemed to have a forlorn quality.

Whenever he had visited in the past, there was always the

screech of the saw, the buzz of the electric press machine, the pounding of the mallet. But today, all was silent. He rang the doorbell.

'Coming,' Nao called as she came to the door. Ayumi had only seen her in check kitchen aprons before, as she went about bookkeeping, filling out payment slips, tapping away at the computer. Today's apron was different. It was plain navy, and the material was thicker than regular household aprons. She was wearing Taisho's work apron, the one he'd used up until a few months ago. Her long hair was cut to shoulder-length, and there was a clarity in her expression that wasn't there the last time he saw her.

'I'm sorry about the sudden visit a few months ago,' Nao apologized as she led him inside and brought him a cup of tea. Okusan was out making a delivery today.

'No, I just wish I could have done more to help.'

'Oh no, I'm glad we could talk. It's nice to talk to someone about my father.'

Only a few months had passed, but Taisho's presence seemed to have faded slightly in the workshop, in the way the tools were positioned, the lumber was leaned against the wall and the papers were stacked.

Ayumi went back and forth in his mind about when to bring up the go-between. As he lifted his head nervously, Nao said, 'Shibuya-san. Can I show you something?'

She brought over a wooden toy. It was a dog with a string for a child to tug on. Ayumi remembered it.

No kid will go for this, right?

'I made this,' Nao said.

Ayumi widened his eyes. *So that's why*, he thought, suddenly understanding. Taisho had spoken so ambiguously about it that day, saying it *might* be a new product. And Ayumi had felt that the toy didn't seem like a creation by Taisho; there were oversights he would never have allowed. But what he found most peculiar was Taisho's tone when he spoke about it. He wasn't someone who criticized toys. Any toy. But he'd been hard on this one – because it was his daughter's creation.

The other toys included the colourful block puzzle, a whale-shaped pushcart, and the rolling ball structure that Ayumi had complimented.

'Did you make all of these?'

'Yes. I'm a little embarrassed to show them to you.'

'Can I take a look?'

'Sure,' Nao said hesitantly.

They were well made and bursting with colour. Ayumi could see how they might capture a child's imagination.

'I showed these to my father. As a kind of test,' Nao said. 'Every single day I watched him work, and I used his designs as inspiration. I wanted to make a few toys that I could show him, to see if he would approve. I was hoping to surprise him.'

'He must have been so surprised.'

'No,' she smiled sadly, shaking her head. 'I think he knew what I was doing, even though I tried to work when he wasn't around. He caught me making something once and told me I needed to let it go. When I took these to him, he just glanced at them and said, "OK I'll take a look."'

'Maybe he didn't want you to see how proud he felt.'

Ayumi couldn't imagine that Taisho wouldn't have been overjoyed. The toys were thoughtfully made, making him think about the amount of trial-and-error they had been through.

'I think your father saw these, and he thought he could trust you with the studio. Don't you think that's why he invited you to go see the trees?'

How he wished they had been able to have that conversation. Even if it didn't change the fact that Taisho was no longer here, Nao would have been able to live on knowing her father believed in her.

'About that. I think I know what my father wanted to tell me.'

'Really?'

'Here. Can you look at this dog?' Nao said, handing him the toy.

Ayumi noticed that the tail with the ball at the end was gone, and instead, a small sphere was attached directly to the soft curve of the dog's bottom.

'I found this in his office after I saw you in Tokyo. The one I made had a hanging tail with a little ball on the end.'

Ayumi remembered saying to Taisho the tail needed to be changed.

'I think my father made this adjustment so the ball wouldn't fall off and be swallowed by mistake. And the walking movement.'

Ayumi wound up the toy and set it on the desk.

'My toy had a more drawn-out motion. But look at how this is just . . . better.'

Ayumi had suggested slowing the movement down, but the toy not only moved slower now, it had a unique rhythm. Whir, flop. Whir, flop. He could picture kids imitating the walk. The movement, the rhythm, the speed – *this* was Taisho.

'I think this was his way of telling me to give up.'

Ayumi turned to her. Her expression had stiffened.

'I think he saw my toy and decided I didn't have what it took.'

Taisho's words came back to him.

No kid will go for this, right?

Talent is a cruel thing. Sometimes people have it and don't know it, and other times, it's just not there.

I've been at this for a long time. Some things you can cover with practice and effort, but nothing can be done about talent. It's a sensibility.

Maybe he'd had Nao in mind. Maybe he was trying to judge, as objectively as possible, whether his daughter was suited to do the work.

Nao picked up the dog. 'And this handle.' She held the back of the dog's head and turned it towards Ayumi. There was an oval-shaped hole that wasn't there before. 'He made this so kids can hold the toy with one hand. It looks completely natural, like it's a part of the dog, but it has a proper function. I could never come up with that,' Nao murmured. 'I saw this and the message was loud and clear. I could never do what he did.'

'He spoke highly of the block puzzle,' Ayumi blurted out. Nao looked at him, surprised, and he stammered, 'I'm sorry. I didn't know these were yours. But I remember Taisho saying this was a good toy. I even asked if he would allow our company to take it on. And he said—'

I may take you up on that someday. I can't make any promises, but if the time comes, I'll let you know.

Nao set the toy down, clasped her hands together and said without emotion, 'Thank you, Shibuya-san. But . . .' She shook her head. 'The puzzle you just complimented, and the rolling ball structure, and the pushcart . . . my father made improvements to all of them. He not only made them more functional, he also improved the design.'

Ayumi didn't know what to say.

'Which is why,' Nao said, 'I'm not giving up.' There was an unwavering gleam in her eyes.

'He was probably going to tell me to give it up. He was going to show me the trees and the lumber and the work of true professionals and tell me not to waste their precious material,' Nao said. 'But when I saw the toys he'd fixed, I thought, I *can't* give up. I mean, I could never do what he did. I know full well that I lack talent. But look at these. Knowing that with a few small adjustments, the toys can transform into this . . . I just . . . we can't close Torino Workshop. I have to do everything I can to protect it. And one day, I *will* catch up to him.' She continued, 'I'm not closing down the studio. We may have to take a break for a few years while I learn the craft. I've contacted a woodworking company that my dad used to work with to see if I can learn from them for a few years. But after that, I hope to open the studio again.'

Ayumi had never heard her speak with such lucidity.

He couldn't move or say anything. What could he do? This family doesn't need the go-between. Some things can be understood without having to see and ask someone a question face-to-face. Sometimes, the things that people left behind spoke more eloquently than any number of words.

Nao already had everything that she needed in order to make her decision.

'I'm sorry for making you come all this way today. But I really wanted to show these to you.' She looked at him. 'Without my father, Torino Workshop may not be worth your time. I'm an amateur when it comes to woodworking, and I know it's a lot to ask. But I hope you won't forget about our studio. I promise we'll be back someday.'

'Of course,' Ayumi nodded.

She patted the toy dog and looked at Ayumi. 'For the past few months, whenever I make something, I always think, what would he do? Or, wow, he's going to yell at me to start over. I think the Dad who lives inside of me is harder on me than in real life.'

Every day I think about what he would do in my situation. I almost wish he would come and yell at me for doing it wrong.

When Ayumi first took over the job of go-between, he couldn't ignore the niggling feeling that wanting to call up the dead was a selfish act on the part of the living. But he had come around to thinking that, for a living person, believing that their loved one is watching them from afar provides strength, in some cases even helping them decide on a path.

Anna was right. Nao didn't need the go-between. Perhaps

in the future, there may come a time when she wished to reunite with her father; when she had grown as an artist and was surrounded by her own creations.

'Do you have ideas of things you want to make?' he asked Nao.

'I do,' she said immediately. 'There's so much I want to try. I'm mad that these were all I had to show my dad. That these few toys were what he based his judgement on!'

Before saying goodbye, Ayumi walked over to the Buddhist altar to pay his respects to Taisho. He lit an incense stick and put his hands together, then looked at Taisho's photograph and said silently, 'You lose.' He and Taisho both. 'Your daughter is an astounding person. I feel stupid for thinking that she needed me to worry about her.'

As he stood to leave, Nao said, 'Please come again. My father always looked like he was having so much fun when he talked to you.'

'It was always just me asking him for advice.'

'Do you think?' Nao tilted her head. 'That's not true. My dad used to say to us, "Ayumi asks me about the colouring and design. Can't believe he wants my advice." He says people of his generation try to do everything on their own and refuse to ask for help.'

Young people these days even ask what colour a product

188

should be. Times really have changed. Back in our day, we had to decide everything for ourselves.

Ayumi turned to look at Taisho's smiling face. He too had to trust in the Taisho that he knew, to believe in the things that he had left behind.

Asking someone directly didn't always land you with the necessary answer. He'd been arrogant to assume that a meeting with the deceased would solve a person's problems.

'Thanks for having me. I'll be back soon,' Ayumi said.

'You're always welcome here,' Nao smiled.

Winter was fast approaching, and soon this area would be covered in snow. It was starting to get dark, and a glimmering round moon hung in the sky. It was almost the next full moon.

Seven years had passed since he took over as the go-between. And for the first time in who knows how long, he had no meetings scheduled.

5

How to Hold Someone in Your Heart

'CAN I ASK you to pass on an additional message this year?'

The man asked as they were about to part ways. Nobody had ever asked that question before. 'Yes?' Ayumi turned.

'Can you please tell Miss Ayako that the rascal Hachiya has turned eighty-five?'

The old man smiled softly.

'DID YOU SAY Germany?' Ayumi asked.

'Yes,' Nao replied.

They were sitting across from each other at a cafe near Ayumi's office. The sunlight flowing in through the window signalled that winter was nearly over; spring was around the

191

corner. According to this morning's reports, the cherry blossoms were expected to start blooming within the next week.

It was not news to Ayumi that Nao was planning to apprentice with a woodworking studio to hone her toymaking skills, and that she would need to close Torino Workshop for a while.

What he didn't expect to hear was that she would do it in Germany.

Last week, when Nao called and said, 'I'll be in Tokyo for work next week. Do you have time for a cup of coffee?' he'd assumed she wanted to discuss next steps regarding her father's studio.

'A woodcraft studio in Nuremberg offered to let me apprentice with them starting in the fall,' she announced. Ayumi blinked. He hadn't imagined she would be leaving the country.

'My father really enjoyed working with them. They're a much bigger studio than we are and have a longer history, but the owner liked my father's work and even visited Karuizawa a few times. They were good friends, so I got up the nerve to ask if I could come and study under them, and they kindly said yes.'

'How long are you thinking of going?'

'It depends,' Nao smiled shyly. 'If I'm decent at the craft and pick things up quickly, it might not be for very long, but I have a feeling I'll need to be there for a while. I want to absorb everything I can.' She gave a nervous laugh. 'The owner of the studio was kind when I met him as my father's friend, but I'm sure it'll be different when I start working under him. He knows mediocre won't cut it if I'm hoping to take over my father's studio. I'm expecting him to be tough.'

Nao spoke without hesitation, her anticipation greater, apparently, than her fear of travelling overseas alone. Even if she was trying to appear more self-assured than she was. For the umpteenth time, Ayumi thought, *She's ten steps ahead of me.*

'That's really great,' he said. Nao was taking off to another country and there was no saying when she would return. But this was a crucial step in her career, a moment he wanted to celebrate with her. 'Germany is a world leader in wooden toys, and there are so many great studios and manufacturers in Nuremberg. What an opportunity. Congratulations.'

'Thank you.'

'I'm sure you'll be swamped before you go. I was hoping to discuss the possibility of turning your puzzle into a product for our company, but . . .'

'What! Are you serious?'

'Yes.'

Ayumi had received his boss's approval to make an official

offer to Nao on the wooden puzzle she'd made, the one that came in various shapes and colours. He had been waiting for the right moment to bring it up, but he now regretted not approaching her sooner.

'Wow,' Nao said, her eyes softening. 'I'd love to hear more about it. Possibly get it going by the fall. I think my mother can work with other local studios on the production side.'

'Great, I'm glad to hear it. OK, I'll come to you and your mother with a formal proposal.' Ayumi was relieved to learn that he would still be working with Nao. Though he wanted to cheer her on in her new endeavour, he couldn't imagine the Karuizawa studio without her.

They walked out of the cafe, and Ayumi was about to say goodbye when Nao said, 'Do you have time to drop by K Garden? I would love to see your turtle in the store.'

'Of course,' he said a beat late. He'd been caught off-guard.

The morning he learned of Taisho's passing, Ayumi was in the toy store at K Garden, taking photos of the new product he had hand-delivered himself. Nao remembered the photos he'd sent to her family.

They headed to the store, where Ayumi introduced Nao to the shop clerk. Learning who she was, the clerk smiled and said, 'It's selling really well.'

There were fewer turtles left on the shelves than the last time Ayumi was here, and one had been set out as a sample toy for children to play with. A child of about two or three was pressing on the turtle shell now.

'Look at him,' Nao whispered as she watched. Ayumi too was moved to see the child take the toy wondrously into his small hands.

As they were leaving the store, Nao's eyes landed on the wooden kitchen play set near the entrance. The imported product was one of the store's top sellers, its toy knife thoughtfully designed to recreate the sharp-edge feel of a real kitchen tool.

'The studio I'm going to in the fall made this.'

'You're going to *this* studio?'

'Yes,' Nao smiled. 'It's exciting to see their products so far from where they were made.'

As they strolled through the shopping centre, Nao said that she was dropping by the bookstore. Ayumi wasn't in any rush, so he decided to tag along. He followed her to the section of the bookstore with the language learning books.

'I need to start studying German,' she said.

Compared to English language books, there were few books for learning German. She reached for a book on a higher shelf.

'I'll grab it. Which one?'

'Oh, sorry, thanks. The one with the brownish spine?'

'This one.'

As Ayumi handed her the book, he heard someone say, 'Oh.' He turned to see an elegant older woman with jewelled glasses and a colourful scarf around her neck.

It was Tokiko Ogasawara. He had helped her reunite with her daughter last year. His body stiffened. He hardly ever ran into people he'd met as the go-between. As he stood frozen, Tokiko looked from him to Nao and gave a wordless nod, so subtle that Nao may not have noticed. The elderly woman walked right past Ayumi and said to Nao, 'Are you studying German?'

'Pardon me? Uh, yes. I hope to.'

'In that case, I don't recommend that one. It's a bestseller, but if you want to learn to speak the language, I recommend that one,' she said, pointing to another book high on the shelf of German books. She looked at Ayumi.

'I'm sorry, can you?'

'Uh, sure.'

Ayumi extended his arm and pulled the book off the shelf. He handed it to Tokiko, who flipped through it and said, 'Yes, this is the one. Here you go,' she said, holding it out to Nao. 'This one was my favourite. Read it a few times and I think you'll get a feel for the language. Anyway, I'm so sorry to intrude.'

Ayumi remembered that the woman's daughter Eiko had lived in Germany.

'Oh no, thank you so much!' Nao said, bowing her head.

Seeing Ayumi's hesitation, the woman smiled gracefully and tipped her head ever so slightly, then whispered, 'She's lovely.'

She seemed to have got the wrong idea, but before he could correct her, she said, 'Have a wonderful day!' and breezed out of the bookstore.

'She was so kind,' Nao marvelled, once Tokiko had disappeared.

Nao had to have heard the woman's comment. Embarrassed for the both of them, Ayumi simply replied, 'Yes, she was.'

He remembered then – something his grandmother had said to him.

If you ever get married, I hope you'll be able to tell the person everything. That you're the go-between. About your father and mother. Everything.

He shook his head to erase the thought.

Ayumi and Nao parted ways, and as he headed back to the office, his phone – the one the go-between used – vibrated. He recognized the name on the screen.

Shigeru Hachiya.

His first thought was, *He called!* Followed by, *It's that time of year already?* Feeling less nervous than when he normally picked up a call as go-between, Ayumi said, 'Hello, Hachiya-san.'

'Hello,' said a scraggly, elderly voice. 'It's been a long time. How have you been?'

'It *has* been a long time. I'm doing great. How are you?'

The man was someone he could speak to in a relaxed manner, though he couldn't forget that he was a client. Ayumi had known him for almost seven years now, ever since he took over from his grandmother.

'Fine, thank you. I'm pleased to be able to call you,' the man said slowly, courteously. 'I would like to ask again, if I may, to be connected with Miss Ayako.'

'Of course,' Ayumi said, like he did last time. With the phone to his ear, he looked up and spotted a few buds on the tree branches. As always, it was the time of year in spring when the cherry blossoms were just about to bloom. 'Let's give it a try.'

Hachiya had requested a meeting with the same person numerous times, and each time, he had been declined.

'Thank you,' the man said calmly.

*

AYUMI FIRST LEARNED about Hachiya when he was training to become the go-between. He was still in high school then, and the season, of course, was spring.

His grandmother was teaching Ayumi how to use the mirror, communicate with the deceased, talk to living clients. She'd shared examples of past cases, though all reunions took place under extraordinary circumstances and no two situations were alike.

One day, his grandmother said, 'I think it's time I told you about Hachiya-san.'

'Hachiya . . . san?'

'I have a feeling he will call this year. You and I can go see him together when he does.'

Ayumi stared at her blankly, and she told him about the man who continued to make the same request, no matter how many times he was turned down.

'Seriously?'

Ayumi had assumed the dead never declined a request. If a living person was able to find their way to the go-between, a difficult thing in itself, didn't that mean the meeting was meant to happen? Those who were not destined to have a meeting weren't able to reach the go-between at all. Right?

'I didn't think people ever got turned down . . .'

'Of course they do,' his grandmother replied matter-of-factly.

'But what's the point of connecting with the go-between if the meeting's not going to happen?'

'Sometimes getting turned down helps resolve something for the client. I've seen it happen before, where people learn their request has been declined, and that helps them find closure in a way that only they can understand.'

Of the deceased who turned down requests, some gave Aiko a specific reason, while others explained nothing. Either way, his grandmother never relayed the reason to the client unless she was asked.

When people learned they had been denied, some begged to know the reason why, while others replied, 'Really?' and let out a sigh of relief.

'You mean finding out they were turned down was enough for them?'

'Possibly. Nobody has ever got angry with me when I told them they've been declined.'

'Angry how?'

'Oh, calling the go-between a scam, for example. Accusing me of having no intention to set them up in the first place.' His grandmother gave a playful laugh. 'These people know better than anyone why their request was declined.'

But Hachiya's situation was different, apparently. As far as Aiko knew, he was the only person who returned again and again with the same request, even after numerous rejections.

'Who does this guy want to see? A family member? Partner? Someone else?'

'I'm not sure,' his grandmother said, tilting her head. 'Why don't you ask him directly? I suspect his request will be coming in soon. It's the third year.'

'The third year?'

'The first time he made a request, he was in his forties, and he came every five years after that. But since he turned seventy, he's been coming every three years. And this is the third year.'

How old was this person? He'd been making the same request from his forties into his *seventies*?

'I'm sure it's hard for you to imagine, but as you get older, you start to think not only about making a request but about becoming the one who is requested. Five years becomes much too long to wait. If he could, he might make the request every year, but perhaps he doesn't want to bother the young lady too much. He has his rules.'

Ayumi noticed she said 'young lady'. But his grandmother only laughed and said, 'You'll see. The request always comes right before cherry blossom season.'

As predicted, Hachiya called that spring. Ayumi and his grandmother met him in a Japanese restaurant that had an elegant courtyard with a single cherry blossom tree.

*

AYUMI OPENED THE door to Hachiya, a *ryotei*, or traditional Japanese restaurant, in Tokyo's historic Kagurazaka area.

That spring night seven years ago when he first accompanied his grandmother here, he'd gawked, 'Are you sure we're supposed to be here?' The looming, old-fashioned residence that had been converted into a restaurant was nothing short of magnificent. As he hesitated at the entrance, his grandmother nudged him and said, 'Go inside.'

The go-between normally specified the meeting location, but Hachiya had been inviting Ayumi's grandmother to meet at the restaurant that shared his name since their very first meeting.

They were led to a private dining room on the second floor. Private rooms in *ryotei* were often tatami-floored spaces with low tables, accompanied by a view of the Japanese garden – complete with the calming sound of a bamboo fountain. But they were led to a modern space with a table and stylish leather chairs. A lovely flower arrangement sat atop the table.

They did have a view of a small courtyard, in which there stood a single tree. 'Cherry blossoms,' his grandmother said. 'When it blooms, the view is sublime.'

Even with only one tree, Ayumi could see that the yard was meticulously cared for.

Some years had passed since that day. A woman in a kimono greeted Ayumi at the entrance as she had last time. 'Welcome back. We've looked forward to your visit.' She led him to the familiar room upstairs. This was Ayumi's second time coming alone.

Shigeru Hachiya was the owner of the long-running restaurant. He'd spent years in the kitchen as head chef, though he was retired by the time Ayumi made his first visit. Before opening Hachiya in Tokyo, he'd spent years training at a renowned *ryotei* in Kyoto, where he remained until his mid-thirties, when he took over this building and converted it into a restaurant.

'Pardon me,' Ayumi said as he entered. Hachiya was waiting for him. He looked at Ayumi and smiled.

'Thank you for coming. I'm sorry to make you travel all this way each time.'

'No, it's my pleasure. Thank you for calling.'

The first time Ayumi saw Hachiya, he was reminded of a gentle, lovable dog, with his fluffy white hair and bushy eyebrows. The old man's eyes squinted behind his glasses as though he were gazing into a bright light, and his expression was always warm. If not a furry dog, maybe a sheep, Ayumi thought. When he saw an Old English Sheepdog on the street one day, he said without thinking, 'Hachiya-san.'

The elderly man seemed slightly smaller than the last time Ayumi saw him. He was not a large man to begin with, but *fluffy* no longer seemed an accurate descriptor. Hachiya waited for Ayumi to take a seat before signalling to the woman in the kimono, 'Please start, thank you.'

'Of course,' she replied, then closed the door softly.

It had become something of a ritual for Ayumi to hear Hachiya's story over a few dishes in this private dining room. The first year, Ayumi took a small bite of the steamed shrimp dumpling containing diced pieces of sweet bamboo shoot, served in a clear dashi broth, and was struck by how delicious it was. 'Oh wow, this is unbelievable,' he'd remarked as his grandmother and Hachiya laughed.

'Isn't it?' his grandmother said. 'That's why I always take Hachiya-san up on his offer to meet here. We're not supposed to become friendly with clients, but how can I say no? It's much too delicious to turn down.'

His grandmother had used the word 'friendly', but both she and Hachiya maintained a respectful distance, never becoming too casual with one another. Hachiya likely did not know his grandmother's name. He must have known that Ayumi was her grandson, but he never mentioned that either.

'How is the previous go-between doing?' he had asked the last time, when Ayumi came alone.

'She passed away last year.'

'Oh,' Hachiya let out a sigh, closing his eyes. He then bowed his head. 'I'm sorry. I didn't know.'

The final dish that day was a smooth *kuzukiri* dessert dipped in brown sugar syrup. It had been his grandmother's favourite.

On Ayumi's way out, Hachiya had said, 'Please take this home with you,' and handed him a small cherry blossom branch wrapped in *washi* paper. A few buds on the branch were on the brink of opening. Ayumi understood the gift to be an offering for his grandmother. Hachiya was a sincere, honourable man.

When his request didn't come in the previous year, Ayumi had been concerned. Hachiya seemed to read his mind.

'I had surgery last year. It was nothing serious. I just needed to have some fluid removed from my lungs. Which is why I wasn't able to contact you.'

'I had no idea,' Ayumi said, his voice tinged with worry.

But Hachiya only laughed. 'I'm sorry if I scared you. I was thinking, I wouldn't blame him if he thought I'd croaked.'

'I didn't think that, but I *was* a little worried. I'm happy that you called this year.'

The first item served tonight was a clear dashi soup with clams and pieces of fish cake, but Ayumi could tell from his seat that Hachiya's pieces were much smaller. Perhaps he was still recovering from his surgery.

'As always, the person I wish to see is Miss Ayako Sodeoka,' Hachiya said as he placed a framed photograph on the table. It was a group photo of people in an array of garments, some in traditional *hakama* and others in Western suits, standing in front of the restaurant where Hachiya had trained early in his career.

'I've explained this to you before, but that's me right there. I worked at a *ryotei* in Kyoto called Sodeoka.'

Young Hachiya stood at one end of the group, next to a few other cooks wearing white kimonos. 'Miss Ayako' sat in the centre between a *hakama*-clad man with a full moustache and an elegant woman in a kimono. She wore her long black hair down and was staring straight into the camera. The photograph was said to have been taken a few years after the war. Nobody smiled in the photo.

'Quite lovely, isn't she? But my, what a fiery personality she had. She was what you might call a beautiful rebel.'

'Right.'

Ayako reminded Ayumi of a Japanese doll, and he couldn't tell from the photo alone whether she was fiery. On the contrary, her delicate features made her seem fragile, vulnerable.

'Ayako was . . .' Hachiya began. 'She was born with some health conditions, and she couldn't attend school like other people her age. She wasn't allowed to run around outside, so she often came into the kitchen where we were preparing

206

meals. She and I were the closest in age, so we became rather friendly. I was eighteen. She must have been about fourteen.'

'Right.'

Ayumi finished his soup, and Hachiya gently placed the lid on his own bowl. He'd hardly taken a sip.

'When I say friendly, well, we weren't allowed to become friends with just anybody back then. I was the third-born son to a family in the mountains of Izumo, and because there was not much for me to do at home, I had to leave and find work. I was fortunate to have been taken in as an apprentice at Sodeoka. They allowed me to stay even after the war ended and the world as we knew it had changed. I was grateful to have a place to go. I was by no means in a position to become friends with the only daughter of the owner of an esteemed restaurant frequented by wealthy clientele and commissioned US military officials. But the owner and his wife were very kind. They felt pity for Miss Ayako because she was unable to leave the house on her own, and they often asked me to accompany her on short outings.'

Hachiya squinted into the distance. 'They asked me to escort Miss Ayako when visiting a friend, and I would carry her bags when she went shopping. Her parents wanted her to enjoy the freedom of buying what she wished. Of course, we're not talking about expensive kimonos or anything of that sort. Though the restaurant was a highly regarded establishment, their best chefs had been taken by the war and they were by no means affluent. The things Miss Ayako purchased were more like assortments of delicate origami paper. She would say, "Here, Hachiya, you can have some," and give me a few sheets of the decorative paper. "Your mother would like this, wouldn't she?" she would say. She was always brusque with me, but when I look back at that time, I see only kindness.'

Ayumi had heard the story numerous times, but he never tired of it. With each telling, 'Miss Ayako' became a livelier, more vibrant character. When Hachiya imitated her, his voice took on a high-pitched, spirited Kyoto dialect, which Ayumi enjoyed.

'I was very fond of Ayako. As embarrassing as it is to say out loud, I do believe it was what one might now call a crush.'

'Right.'

'It is of course not surprising that my feelings were not reciprocated, as we were of unequal standing – it was a different time then. I never expected that anything would happen between us, nor did I think to act on my feelings. It had been decided since she was a girl that she would marry one Shoji Miyajima. He was the second son of the owner of a renowned *ryotei* in Osaka, and once Miss Ayako turned seventeen, he was to marry into her family and in the future take over Sodeoka. Miss Ayako would often boast to her friends, "Shoji will be by my side soon." She was very muchlooking forward to it. I accompanied her to Osaka once to see him.'

'That must have been hard for you,' Ayumi said, though his thinking might have been too contemporary for the time.

'Oh no,' he shook his head, appearing happy to have been asked. 'It is indeed a strange thing, but it filled me with joy to see Miss Ayako with Shoji. They were a lovely couple, and I felt their bliss when I was near them. But then . . .' Hachiya's tone grew heavy. 'Ayako passed away when she was sixteen, before she and Shoji could marry. It was very, very unfortunate.'

Ayako had suffered from severe asthma since she was a young girl. When Hachiya first met her, he was shocked by how pale she was, her arms and legs as fragile as glass.

'She may have had other illnesses aside from her asthma. To think that if she had the medical care available to us now, she could have lived a much longer life. She was so young. Her mother and father were devastated, saying they had let her die alone. Her mother, especially, fell into a deep sorrow.'

'Right.'

'With marriage no longer an issue, the *ryotei* was succeeded by the head chef, whom I trained under. I continued to work at the restaurant for some time after, and then in my mid-thirties, I opened this place. But I kept in close touch with the owner and his wife for years after. When I close my eyes, I can remember every detail of the restaurant and their house. Both are filled with memories of Miss Ayako. That was my entire youth. All of early adulthood.'

Hachiya sat up. He opened his eyes wide and looked at Ayumi.

'Mr Go-Between. I have been requesting a meeting with Miss Ayako for many years, and I do have a good understanding of why she has not said yes. She too has only one opportunity to see someone, after all. *Why would I use it on Hachiya? I can hear her now. That boy needs to know his place.*'

'But you would still like to see her?'

'Yes.' He gave a firm nod, then laughed. 'Though I'm sure she will turn me down again.'

'Right,' Ayumi said as the next item arrived. A delicious aroma filled the room. He peered into the dish and saw something like mochi with a small dollop of wasabi on top. *I know this aroma . . . sakura,* he thought.

'It's sakura rice cake steamed with sea bream. Please enjoy it while it's hot.'

'Thank you.'

'I think you've now had everything on our spring menu. What will we serve you next time?' the elderly man asked in a light tone, though it made Ayumi's chest ache to know he was already thinking about next time.

Hachiya's requests always came right before the cherry blossoms bloomed, the timing of which shifted each year. Ayumi guessed that Ayako might have passed away around this time of year.

After the meal, Hachiya walked Ayumi down to the entrance. He appeared to move slower than before, his footing less steady on the stairs. 'This restaurant is very similar,' the old man said as they were halfway down the stairs, 'to the main house where Miss Ayako lived. They too had a cherry tree in their backyard.'

Ayumi looked at the lone tree outside of the window. Hachiya spoke in the past tense; perhaps the house no longer existed.

'When the previous owner of this building asked if I was interested in opening a restaurant here, I was ready to turn him down. I'd been in Kyoto for so long at that point, I assumed that if I were to open a restaurant, it would be in that city. But when I visited this location, I fell instantly in love.' He shifted his gaze from the window to Ayumi. 'I'd heard rumours about the go-between before, but I never imagined I would make a request myself. But a few years after starting this restaurant, I had the sudden impulse. Perhaps a part of me wished to show Miss Ayako that I was now standing on my own two feet. When I heard she had refused, I wasn't surprised. I don't deserve a one-on-one meeting with her.' He looked at Ayumi. 'Mr Go-Between, can I ask you to pass on an additional message this year?'

This was new. 'Yes?'

'Can you please tell Miss Ayako that the rascal Hachiya has turned eighty-five?'

The old man smiled softly. 'That is all you need to say. Thank you.'

'ISN'T AYAKO THAT super self-centred girl I've heard a lot about?' Anna asked. 'So the request came this year, huh.'

'Self-centred?'

'That's how she sounds from your stories!' Anna pouted. 'Why won't she just say yes?'

When it came time to negotiate with the deceased, a key task for the go-between, Ayumi often used the Akiyamas' backyard. He had come over for the ritual tonight and had run into Anna.

'Hey, can you listen to me read out loud for my homework?'

Anna's parents were out tonight. On her homework sheet was a column for the guardian to check off, once the student completed the assigned task. 'I *could* check the box myself, but since you're here.'

As she read aloud from her textbook, Ayumi checked off

the boxes for: volume, reading speed and posture. Of course, this was Anna, practically a professional. She enunciated perfectly, like a child actor auditioning for a part. Like she said, her teacher would never know the difference whether she did the homework or not. But maybe she *wanted* Ayumi to hear her read.

'Hachiya-san knows there's someone Ayako wants to see more than him. Still, he can't help but wish for a reunion with her.'

'I mean, I guess . . .'

Though Ayumi rarely shared the details of a client request with Anna's parents, he often found himself confiding in Anna. He filled her in, both because she was the head of the household, which meant he could trust her with the information, and because she was a good listener.

When Hachiya didn't call last year and Ayumi worried that something might be wrong, Anna had told him, 'Chill out. He'll probably call next year.' She reminded him of his grandmother in many ways. Now that his grandmother was gone, he viewed Anna as advisor to the go-between.

'But aren't you glad?' Anna asked.

'Hmm?'

'That he called this year.'

'Yeah.'

He thought about how Hachiya had seemed smaller, and

wondered if his requests would start coming every other year, or even every year. Ayumi could sense that the old man felt he was running out of time. Surely that's what he meant when he said, 'Can you please tell Miss Ayako that the rascal Hachiya has turned eighty-five?'

'Why do you look so down today anyway?'

'Huh?'

Anna's eyes bore into him, her expression uncharacteristically serious.

'I'm not . . . down . . .'

'Seems that way.'

Could it be because of the news Nao had delivered earlier?

'You OK?' she asked.

'I'm good,' he replied.

'OK. By the way, I have a question. I'm asking generally.' She cast her gaze away, which wasn't like her. 'If a boy gets a gift for Valentine's Day, do they give something back, even if they don't like that person? How was it for you?'

Ayumi widened his eyes. 'What, you mean . . .'

'I said it was a general question. It's not about me!' She turned away.

Anna was growing up too.

In one corner of the Akiyama garden along a row of mossy rocks lay a round, flat rock with a dip at its centre. On rainy days it filled with rainwater, and seeing the moonlight shine on the water's surface one night, Ayumi decided that the rock was ideal for placing the mirror when performing his ritual.

The woman appeared again wearing an exquisite kimono, just like in the photograph.

'Ms Ayako Sodeoka,' Ayumi called, and she cocked her head and glanced his way. Her fringe was cut in a straight line above her eyebrows, giving her the look of a Japanese doll. She blinked slowly, as if to communicate that the light was too bright.

She raised her annoyed eyes at Ayumi, and after a pause, she finally opened her mouth. 'Oh, you again,' she said dully.

Quite lovely, isn't she? But my, what a fiery personality she had. She was what you might call a beautiful rebel.

Don't I know it, thought Ayumi. Through his numerous encounters with her, he knew the woman was nothing like she appeared in the photograph Hachiya had shown him.

'Shigeru Hachiya would like a meeting with you—'

'No,' she said before he could finish. 'I thought I told you. I don't know what makes Hachiya think he can request a meeting with me.'

'I understand,' said Ayumi. It was against the rules to become emotionally invested in either party, and as much as Ayumi wanted to help Hachiya, he was careful not to step over the line. 'I'm sorry to have bothered you.'

'Do you know how much of a hassle this is? Coming all this way, for Hachiya of all people?' she snapped.

Ayumi felt like running and hiding himself, but he had promised the old man. 'I have an additional message today from Mr Hachiya. I am going to say it in his exact words. "Can you please tell Miss Ayako that the rascal Hachiya has turned eighty-five?"'

Ayumi wasn't able to make out Ayako's expression. He waited, but there was no response. 'Thank you. I will let him know your answer.'

As he reached for the mirror, he heard, 'Wait!'

Ayumi pulled his hand back. The young woman turned to him slowly, her brows furrowed. She no longer appeared bored or irritated.

'Hachiya's eighty-five?' she said timidly, almost child-like. She *was* only sixteen.

Ayumi hadn't given much thought before to how time must have passed – or stopped – for her. Time never slowed down for the living and the old man's requests had spanned several decades, but for Ayako, they may have come in quick succession. Maybe she wasn't aware of how much time had passed since her death.

'Yes.'

After a long silence, she said, 'I'll see him.'

Ayumi widened his eyes. Ayako repeated, 'I said I'll see

him. Tell Hachiya that.' She was back to sounding bored, just as Anna had earlier when she was trying to hide her discomfort.

WOULD HE BE thrilled or speechless? Ayumi wondered. But Hachiya was strangely calm.

'Is that so? She said yes,' he said before exhaling quietly.

'The meeting will be held at a hotel in Shinagawa. Are you available the night of the next full moon? We will have a room ready.'

For the first time, Hachiya's voice wavered slightly. 'Is there any possibility that I might be able to choose the meeting place?'

'I'm sorry, but the meeting must be held in a specific location.'

Did Hachiya hope to meet with Ayako at his restaurant? Because it was similar to the home she grew up in? Ayumi wished he could accommodate the old man's request, but according to his grandmother, the hotel in Shinagawa was situated in the direct path of the full moon, which was a requirement for the deceased to appear.

'I see.' Hachiya now sounded openly worried. 'I understand. Thank you. Please give Miss Ayako my regards.'

The next morning, the man called back. 'I'm sorry, but I have another enquiry regarding the meeting place.'

'Yes?' Ayumi braced himself.

'Would it be possible to reserve a room on one of the lower floors? The first and second floors of the hotel are restaurants and banquet halls, and guest rooms begin on the third floor. Room 309 or 317 would be ideal.'

Ayumi didn't have an answer. No client had asked for a specific room before. 'Uh, OK, yes. I'll check to see if that's possible.'

'Thank you.' Ayumi imagined Hachiya bowing on the other end of the line. 'The night of the next full moon looks clear,' the old man said. 'I'm looking forward to it.'

His voice sounded upbeat, as though the joy had finally caught up to him.

AS PREDICTED, THE night of the meeting was clear.

The highly anticipated cherry blossoms were in full bloom, and spotlights illuminated the cherry trees surrounding the hotel. Guests and non-guests alike strolled the hotel premises, taking in the spectacular nighttime view of the pink and white petals.

Hachiya showed up in a white spring jacket and bluish-grey

flat cap. He always dressed stylishly, but today he appeared younger and more dashing than usual. He swept into the hotel lobby without the help of a cane.

'Thank you for your time today,' he said and bowed as soon as he saw Ayumi.

'I was able to reserve Room 309 as requested. She is awaiting your arrival now.'

Hachiya's expression tightened. This was the moment he'd been waiting for. For years. Decades.

'You have from now until dawn. When you've finished, please come down to the lobby. I'll be waiting there.'

'Yes, about that, Mr Go-Between . . . is there any way this old geezer can ask for one last favour? Please.'

'A favour?'

'Do you think there is any possible way that you can join me?'

'What?' Ayumi didn't mean to say it so loudly.

'That's asking too much,' Hachiya said.

'It's not that. It's just . . . this is the moment you've been waiting for. You don't want me to be there. Do you?'

He could see that Hachiya's hands, in prayer position in front of his chest, were trembling. The old man balled them into tight fists, but now, both fists shook violently.

'I'm quite scared,' Hachiya said, forcing a smile. 'I know I am not who Miss Ayako really wishes to see. And I may find myself unable to speak once I am alone with her. It would mean so much if you could see me through it.'

Though this was unprecedented, Ayumi felt he understood the old man's trepidation. This was the headstrong Ayako they were talking about after all. He glanced at the wrinkles and veins popping out of Hachiya's hands and tried to imagine the fear of letting the young woman see how he had aged.

'If you're sure . . .'

'Thank you.'

Hachiya took Ayumi's hand and squeezed it. His own hands had stopped trembling.

AYUMI INSERTED THE key in the door slot and the green lamp flickered.

As he gestured for Hachiya to go inside, the elderly man nodded and proceeded slowly into the room. Ayumi trailed after him, inching forward as cautiously as possible.

The young woman was seated in front of the mirror.

Hachiya inhaled, making a high whistling sound. Even from behind, Ayumi could feel his shock and exhilaration.

'You're Hachiya?'

Ayako wore a long pale skirt and soft white blouse with

a cameo brooch on the chest. Ayumi had never seen her in anything but a kimono, but maybe it was not uncommon for women in her day to don Western-style garments.

'Miss Ayako!' Hachiya stepped forward. 'It has been a very long time . . . I am indeed . . . Hachiya.'

'Hachiya, you . . . my goodness, you're an old man!'

'Yes, yes, I am, Miss Ayako. I regret to say that I am now quite old.'

'I don't believe it,' Ayako said, shaking her head.

As soon as he heard Ayako's Kyoto dialect, Hachiya switched over too, sounding the way they perhaps had decades earlier. 'I'm sorry to make you come all this way,' he said, the emotion rising in his voice, and Ayako shot him an annoyed glare.

'No kidding. Do you know who you're talking to?'

Watching the two interact, Ayumi felt relief wash over him. Although Ayako's words came out sounding harsh, Hachiya's expression was bright. 'I apologize,' he said with a merry laugh. 'I am sorry for making you come all this way. I'm sorry for being an old fogey.'

'Um . . .' Ayako noticed someone else in the room for the first time.

Ayumi quietly bowed his head, trying to make himself as small as he could.

*

With Ayako's permission, Ayumi poured two cups of tea using the teabags in the room. Ayako and Hachiya sat facing each other across a small table, and Ayumi took a seat on the bed.

'You're eighty-five now,' Ayako spoke first, her eyes regarding the old man hesitantly.

'Yes,' Hachiya said with a warm smile. Now that the initial shock had settled, he seemed to be back to his usual calm self.

'Which means everyone else must be gone. Father and Mother too?'

Hachiya neither nodded nor denied it and only smiled, his eyes soft. She took a deep breath. 'And Sakurako, Junko, Kaoru, and Mifune Sensei.'

The friends she mentioned were probably close to her in age, meaning that they might still be around. But that was not the point. Ayako continued, 'And Shoji.' She lowered her voice. 'Nobody but you wanted to see me.' There was a desperate edge to her voice. 'There's no one left for me to wait for. Right?'

'I'm sure they didn't know about the go-between,' Hachiya finally replied. 'It was only by chance that I learned about the go-between myself. Either that, or I was the only one gullible enough to believe the story.'

'That's a lie. After you learned about the go-between, I'm

sure you told Shoji, didn't you? You asked him to come see me. But he never did.'

Hachiya didn't answer. He was fast becoming a smiling statue.

Watching silently, Ayumi thought about how the deceased often acted as a mirror for the living. Those who requested meetings sought answers about themselves, and they hoped that seeing their loved ones would help them find them. But today, it was the opposite. Ayako seemed to be searching for answers inside the old man. Hachiya, he gathered, knew this, and was accepting of his role.

A tear rolled down Ayako's cheek, and Hachiya took out a handkerchief and handed it to her. She took it and dabbed her eyes.

The old man began to speak.

'I'd been hoping for an opportunity to see you so that I could tell you how things were after your passing. My hope was to see you while I could, which is why I asked the kind go-between to mention that I am now eighty-five.' He looked at Ayako. 'Not a day passed in our lives that your father, mother, friends and teachers, and yes, Shoji too, did not think about you. Your parents were devastated that they had let you go alone, and they were with you every day in spirit. None of us forgot about you. You were never alone.'

Ayako lowered her handkerchief and raised her damp eyes. 'We all wished you were still with us,' Hachiya assured her.

'You sound like a teacher.' Ayako had stopped crying, and she sounded a little more like her usual self.

'My apologies,' Hachiya smiled. 'I have lived much too long. At this age, it's difficult to speak without it coming out like a lecture. Forgive me, Miss Ayako.'

'You had feelings for me, didn't you, Hachiya?' Ayako squinted, ruminating on the past. She sounded almost shy when she said, 'I still remember when you confessed to me that my happiness was your happiness.'

'It was audacious of me. I'm surprised, and moved, that you remember at all.'

'So what was your life like after? When I was no longer around?'

'I continued to train at Sodeoka, and then in my mid-thirties, I opened my own restaurant. I have a restaurant in Tokyo's Kagurazaka area now, called Hachiya. Though I'm no longer in the kitchen myself.'

'Little Hachiya, who was always crying in the corner because the other cooks were so hard on you. Now with your own restaurant?'

'It's hard to believe.'

'And what happened to Sodeoka? I know that the

families decided Shoji would become a part of my family with or without me. Did he end up taking over the restaurant?'

'Kondo, the head chef, ended up taking over. I believe one of his apprentices has now stepped in.'

'What! Why?'

Ayumi was surprised that Hachiya was providing so much detail, but the old man continued to sit coolly.

'He never came to Kyoto to take over the restaurant?'

'I do believe it was for the best. Shoji wasn't cut out to work in the culinary world. He dabbled in it at his parents' restaurant, but he quickly gave up and started a business in finance. I don't know that he would have done well had he taken over Sodeoka.'

'What are you saying?'

'I am saying that is how much he was hoping to marry you. So much that he would commit himself to a business and industry he was ill-suited for.'

'So he never came to Kyoto . . .'

'No.'

'And what about you?' she asked. Her eyes softened. 'Do you have a family? You didn't spend your whole life pining for me, did you?'

'No.' Hachiya smiled sheepishly. 'Shortly after I opened the restaurant in Tokyo, I met and married a woman in an arranged marriage. We had three boys and a girl, and my eldest son now runs the restaurant.'

Ayako widened her eyes and stared at Hachiya. 'Then you ...'

'Yes.'

'You have a full, happy life!'

'I've been very fortunate.'

'Oh, for goodness' sake! You confess your feelings for me, and then you go and live a full and happy life without me!'

'We may have lived full lives, but nobody said they were happy because you were gone,' Hachiya said sharply, catching Ayako by surprise. He stood and walked slowly towards her, then kneeled respectfully before her. 'Your parents, your friends, Shoji and myself . . . We've all gone our separate ways, but each of us wished we could have spent our lives with you. If I had the choice now, even if it meant not having my restaurant or my family, I would choose to live in a world that had you in it. I'm sure everybody else feels the same way. You have and will continue to live in our hearts.' He looked into her eyes. 'That is what I have come here to say.'

'That's why you went to the trouble of requesting me?' The coldness had vanished from her face.

'No. My main reason for requesting you was something else. I wanted you to be able to experience the cherry blossoms one final time.' He turned to Ayumi and smiled. 'May I ask you to open that curtain?'

'Of course.'

Ayumi pressed a button on a remote control and the curtains opened to reveal a night sky illuminated by the full moon and the lit-up cherry blossoms. The trees were lined up right beneath the window.

He finally understood why Hachiya had requested a room on a low floor. Peering down from the window, they had an up-close view of the cherry blossoms in full, breathtaking bloom.

'Ohhhhhh my goodness,' sighed a dreamy voice.

Ayumi didn't recognize the voice as belonging to Ayako. Her face was now plastered to the window as she breathed in the view.

'This is magnificent. Absolutely breathtaking!'

'Yes, it is.'

'Isn't it brilliant, Hachiya?'

'Yes.'

'Are the trees lit from below? I can see the outlines of each flower, as though they've been folded out of origami.'

'Yes.' Hachiya was grinning broadly. 'You were always fond of the flowers.'

Ayumi remembered Hachiya asking if the meeting could be held at his restaurant. The private dining room had a stunning view of the cherry blossom tree in the courtyard.

When Ayako wasn't looking, Hachiya took a small step back from the window and dabbed at his eyes. Ayumi thought he heard him whisper, 'Thank goodness.'

Hachiya didn't choose this time of year because it was when Ayako passed away. He'd chosen it so that she could enjoy the brief but beautiful cherry blossoms.

'Hachiya, do you think that window there has a good view?'

'Yes, yes, I do.'

Hachiya quickly wiped his tears and put his glasses back on as he hurried over.

'Would you like me to order a plate of Sakuramochi?' Ayumi asked, and the pair turned to him in unison. 'I think I saw it on the room service menu. A special item just during cherry blossom season.'

'Oh, that sounds wonderful!' Ayako's eyes sparkled, and though Ayumi wondered for a moment if she knew what room service was, he nodded. 'Coming right up, Miss Ayako.'

Ayumi stayed and enjoyed a night of cherry blossom viewing with the pair. Whenever the elderly Hachiya started to nod off, Ayako cried, 'Wake up!' and tapped him on the cheek. She watched the flowers without ever tiring of them, until finally, the sky began to grow light.

The room service tray that Ayumi ordered had come with a plate of traditional Sakuramochi sweets, sake and a small cherry blossom branch, which delighted Ayako. She held on to it until her final moment.

'Hachiya.'

Ayumi sat back, trying to give them as much space as possible.

'Thank you for this. I didn't think that I would ever be able to experience the cherry blossoms again.'

'Thank you, Miss Ayako,' Hachiya replied. 'I cannot express how grateful I am.'

Ayako smiled. She held out the cherry blossom branch, and as Hachiya took hold of it, she vanished. Nothing was left but the branch.

The old man stared at the spot where Ayako had been standing. His hand, clenching the tree branch, started to tremble. And then shake. Violently. He didn't utter a word. As Ayumi started to walk towards him, Hachiya raised the branch over his head, then collapsed to the floor.

'Hachiya-san!'

Ayumi rushed over to the old man, who was now weeping. 'I'm sorry,' he said, grabbing on to Ayumi's arm. In between sobs, he said, 'She was . . . only . . . sixteen . . . She . . . looked forward to . . . the cherry blossoms each year. She didn't know how much longer . . . she had . . . The wait must have been painful . . . more than any of us could have imagined.'

'Yes, yes,' Ayumi said, supporting the elderly man.

'I just . . . wanted to show her one last time.' Even if it meant showing her that he was no longer the young man she had once known. He was her last hope of ever seeing the blossoms again.

The rascal Hachiya has turned eighty-five.

He was telling her that this was his, and her, last chance. He folded his body in half on the floor and wept.

Ayumi patted the old man's back gently, until he was ready to get back on his feet.

AYUMI WALKED HIS client to a taxi parked in front of the hotel. Before climbing in, Hachiya gave Ayumi a fatigued smile.

'I'm embarrassed by what you saw up there.'

'Please. There is nothing to be embarrassed about.'

'Excuse me for being rude, but are you married, Mr Go-Between?'

'No . . . not yet.'

'I see. One day, when you find that person, please bring them to my restaurant. It will be my treat.'

'Oh, I couldn't let you . . .'

Now that Hachiya was no longer a client, Ayumi didn't imagine that he would be able to set foot in the restaurant again. It was out of his league. But when he saw Hachiya's kind eyes, he changed his mind.

'When I do visit, I will pay.'

'You know we're pretty expensive.'

'I know,' Ayumi smiled.

Hachiya turned his gaze to the cherry blossoms under the early morning sun.

'It's a gift to live in the world at the same time as the person you have in your heart,' he said, sounding as though he were talking to himself. 'We all kept Miss Ayako in our hearts, but we were never to live with her again.' He turned to look at Ayumi. 'You're still very young. I hope that in your life, you will let your heart lead.'

The man had never spoken to Ayumi in such a personal tone.

'Thank you,' he said. 'I will.'

'I'll see you then,' Hachiya said and climbed into the taxi. Ayumi watched as the car sped down the street lined on both sides with the magnificent but delicate flowers that bloomed for only a week or two each year.

As he headed to the office, Ayumi sent a message from his phone.

Good morning. There's something I'm hoping to talk to you about. Would it be OK if I come to see you in Karuizawa?

He thought she might be sleeping so early in the morning, but she replied right away.

Good morning! Is it about the block puzzle?

Ayumi hesitated, then typed out his reply.

It's not about work, actually. It's something personal. Is that OK?

As he waited nervously for her reply, his grandmother's words came back to him. He had been repeating them in his head, in fact, since the day he ran into Tokiko Ogasawara at the bookstore.

If you get married, I hope you'll be able to tell the person everything. That you're the go-between. About your father and mother. Everything.

If it hadn't been Nao he was with when they ran into Tokiko, Ayumi might have panicked about running into a client. The go-between was his secret life.

But he knew he would eventually reveal the truth. He knew that telling her meant burdening her in many ways, and he didn't need to go into any details right now. Right now, he needed only to tell her one thing.

She might not feel the same way. He was three years younger than her, and perhaps not worthy of her trust. Not to mention that she was about to embark on the most important journey of her career – he didn't want to hold her back.

His grandmother would root him on, he thought. No. She'd yell at him for getting in Nao's way.

A light wind blew, and a few petals flittered off the branches.

His phone vibrated. He tried to control his wildly beating heart as he opened the screen.

Of course! How's next Tuesday?

Ayumi let out the breath he'd been holding.

Perfect. I'll see you then.

He hit *send* and tucked the phone away, then took a step in the direction of the morning sun.

MIZUKI TSUJIMURA is the much-loved author of million-copy-bestselling mystery and puzzlebox novels. *Lost Souls Meet Under a Full Moon* explores our relationship with the memories of deceased loved ones and what gives our lives meaning. It was made into a high-budget Japanese-language film and won a newcomer award. Its sequel, *How to Hold Someone in Your Heart*, was also a huge bestseller, cementing the appeal of Tsujimura's unique combination of emotion, mystery and magic. She is the author of the groundbreaking novel *Lonely Castle in the Mirror*, which was also adapted for anime and manga and which combines real-world fantasy with important themes of mental health and friendship. Tsujimura has won many awards, including the Japan Booksellers' Award and the Naoki Prize, and is published worldwide. English-language editions of many of her works, including *True Mothers* and *Arrogance and Virtue* (now a major Japanese-language film), are due to be published soon.